HUMANS, GODS, AND HYBRIDS

EPISODE 1

Child 19

MARK L. MARINACCIO

HUMANS, GODS, AND HYBRIDS
Episode 1 - Child 19

by Mark L. Marinaccio
www.markmarinaccio.com

Published 2020 by The Strange Story Co.

Library of Congress Control Number: 2020917782
ISBN: 978-0-578-76495-5 (Paperback)
ISBN: 978-0-578-76496-2 (Ebook)

Books may be purchased by contacting
the publisher and author at:

Mark@strangestory.com

Publisher:
The Strange Story Company
Agoura Hills, CA 91301

First Edition Printed in the United States of America

HUMANS, GODS, AND HYBRIDS

EPISODE 1

Child 19

PART 1
KELLAN

Chapter One

SUBTLE, TRIPLE ALARMS chimed inside the moving cabin. Kellan bit back a groan and burrowed his face deeper into his Tendra's shoulder, breathing in her scent. The alarm signaled three things to Kellan: First, it was time to wake up; second, he'd need to put his clothes back on, and third, the lives of nearly eight billion people were about to change forever.

He saw tiny specs of light buried within the sea of darkness shining outside the clear, glass window at the end of the room. For more than twenty years he'd been staring out that window looking for answers. And now it floated before him, in a blue orb, as uncertain as ever before.

Earth.

Since birth he, Tendra, and the others had been staring down at monitors, reading countless texts, and filling their minds with thoughts of Earth. For the entirety of his twenty-two years of life, it was all anyone could talk about. But the time for talking and wondering, the uncertainty was coming to an end, and the time of action and realized expectations was upon him, upon them all.

The glittering starlight dimly filled the cramped interior cabin.

The room resembled the cabin of a classic European passenger train moving through the night. This one moved effortlessly and almost silently except for the slight hum of a distant engine–a reproduction of an antique, perhaps, with perfect, unchipped, wooden accents and Edison bulb fixtures too fresh to be true vintage. There was plasticity to everything, a false cleanliness that revealed newness in place of the scratched and rubbed after effects that came with age and repeated, constant care. The room was large enough for a bed, positioned for optimal viewing of the stars and an abundance of white, silky sheets and even whiter, fluffy pillows.

Kellan ran a hand through his dark hair, pushing it out of his face as he rolled onto his back. He was in solid shape with broad shoulders and powerful arms. As the son of the leader of their people, he had to be strong. His father wouldn't accept anything less. His strength separated him from the rest of the Travelers– well, one of the things that separated them.

Tendra let out a cute, little noise of protest and snuggled into his side.

Tendra was so tiny next to him that she could become lost in his massive embrace. If they were standing, she'd barely come up to his chest. He watched her slender fingers trail up and down his forearm, lighting up his senses and making him shudder. Kellan ran his hand over her smooth, light skin, drawn to her warmth.

Her blonde hair had its share of rebellious red streaks that reflected her fire. Her bright green eyes were the perfect complement to his sky-blue ones. She was the most attractive girl Kellan had ever seen. He called her "Ten" because, in his eyes, she was one.

He adjusted so that she could use his arm as her pillow. He didn't mind an awkward elbow or numb arm if it meant he got to hold her. A content smile pulled at his lips. He could stay here forever with her.

But they couldn't.

His smile quickly faded as the annoying reminder of the audible signals set in.

"Where will we go first once we get there?" Tendra asked, turning her head to look out the window.

Kellan followed her gaze.

"Why go at all? Let *them* leave," he gestured a wave. "Then we'll have the whole place to ourselves," he teased her. Kellan would love to spend their time together aboard their ship as it hovered above humanity. Why leave and face the unknown when they'd managed to find love amongst their limited options of only a few thousand Travelers aboard the ship? Twenty years was a long time to be in one place with the same people, and if not for Tendra, he might feel differently about leaving and exploring, but why risk it when he had all he needed right here in his arms?

They'd had this conversation a thousand times before, and she never wavered. As usual, she started to hum a familiar tune, "Memories" from *Cats the Musical*. She had loved that song for as long as he could remember, going back to when they were children and she'd sit alone in the music room playing it over and over again. It became her obsession. One he'd had to suffer through reenacting the whole musical with her. Even in his sleep, he heard the songs.

Her humming changed, and the words eked out and grew until she eventually turned back toward Kellan, smiling. He knew that she was nervous and trying to lighten the mood. She was just as unsure as he was about what was to come for them.

"Bravo, bravo, <u>bellissimo</u>!"

She giggled, and he felt it vibrate all throughout his body, echoing in his chest. She rested her head against him. "I can't wait to see a Broadway show. The music, the dancing, the lights. Can you imagine me up on the stage, people cheering for me?"

"I don't know how I'd feel sharing those legs with the world. I might get jealous." He tickled her thigh, and she let out a squeal of laughter, wiggling away, before smacking his chest.

He rolled out of bed and held his hand out to her. She wrapped the sheets around her and took his hand, and he pulled her to her feet. He held her close, wrapping his arms around her, and started to sway, pressed together as if separating from each other would have dire consequences.

"I'm going to see a show at night so that I can see all of the lights on Broadway." Her green eyes were wide with excitement. They pulled at him, and all he wanted was to give her whatever she desired.

"How about I put a show on for you?" Kellan spun her away and then pulled her back into his arms, giving her a quick kiss on the nose.

"If we do go down, Alaska sounds nice, if anywhere. There are people there that carve these massive, wooden statues into gigantic, grizzly bears and eagles and wolves. I'd buy one and carry it away on my shoulders back to our little cabin in the middle of the woods, far away from any civilization. That's what I want. Our own oasis away from everyone else. Just you and me."

She placed a chaste kiss on his lips and then slipped out of his arms. She bent to reclaim her undergarments from the floor by the bed.

Kellan held back a sigh. He didn't really know what Alaska would be like, of course. He knew that. Neither did she, though. All that they knew of the world that spun below was what they'd learned in books, on computers, and from the teachers who had only learned from books and computers as well.

"Too bad you're in love with a city girl." Her pinched brows and downcast eyes revealed her contempt for his ideas.

He snorted. "A city girl? Even though you've never been? What if it's too big and scary of a place for you?" His laughter was met with a toddler-like grimace.

"You should get dressed. We should see our friends off." Tendra told him as she slipped on her underwear.

Kellan looked out into the stars. In a few weeks, people would start leaving the ship in small groups of a dozen or so at a time. Thousands would dwindle to hundreds. The once bustling craft would become desolate, and while he'd like the space all to themselves, it would make Tendra restless. She didn't like to wait, and for too long she'd waited to leave the ship. But the fear of the unknown shadowed his thoughts.

Kellan stepped toward her, and her back stiffened. "Ten, we're going to be okay."

Tendra turned to him, her eyes welled with tears, and she blinked them away. "Of course."

"I love you, Ten," he whispered as he stroked her

cheek and pressed his forehead to hers. "I just don't know what it will be like. What if it's not what you hoped? What if they don't accept us?"

She ignored him. "How about California? We can lie in the sun all day, and then be in the mountains at the night. Or we can take a boat up the coast and sleep outside under the stars. That's right up your alley."

He humored her with a small smile. "That sounds perfect."

Her smile faded, her gaze dropped, and her shoulders slumped. "You're lying. You're scared. I know you worry, but there's no reason to think anything will go wrong."

She was right, she knew exactly what he thought.

"Ten, what if it doesn't go as everyone had hoped? What if it's not as fun and exciting as we've read? What if the people are nasty and violent and turn on us like they have done to so many foreigners before, throughout history?"

"I don't see why that would happen to us. We've planned for this. We're being welcomed now. If we do what we are asked and we follow the rules, then we should be free to go wherever we want. America especially is a very welcoming place, it has a history of allowing foreigners in and letting them earn citizenship. They were founded on those principles. Why should we be any different?"

Tendra stared blankly out into the stars.

Kellan hated disappointing her, but she needed to see reason, to see the dangers. She couldn't just ignore the signs and pretend; there was too much at stake.

"Because we *are* different, Ten. We're not just *any* immigrants."

A new, subtle alarm sounded. Anticipation replaced the melancholy. The cabin illuminated, and the low-pitched hum gradually slowed to silence.

An accommodating voice echoed over a loudspeaker, "Travelers, it is my honor and privilege to inform you that our leader, Ringbak Arr, stands alongside the leaders of the world, and at this very moment speaks with them to the entirety of human civilization. Due to the transmission delay, we are expecting to begin streaming the event and his speech any moment. Please find your friends, partners, and loved ones and join us in one of the community viewing rooms in ten minutes. We are now moving into position directly above North America, and the United States."

Tendra's curiosity got the better of her. She raced over to the window and pressed her face against the cold pane beside the bed. "Look, Kellan, there it is!" Kellan sauntered over, standing close behind her. Peering over her shoulder, he saw it, North America; a beautifully frightening patch of brown in a bright blue sea, stuck on an orb in a distant view of darkness.

"It's beautiful," Tendra said in awe.

The sight of Tendra's joy put Kellan on edge. She was being naive. He walked over to grab his pants off the floor, pulled them up, and buttoned them. As he tugged his discarded shirt over his head, his hand grazed the triangle formation of his three protruding belly buttons along his stomach.

"Come on then, let's go see the others," Tendra pressed impatiently.

"Okay, but tonight it's just us, right? No friends. Back here, dinner in bed?"

"Oh, Kel, you know I can't. I'm on duty at the nursery tonight, I told you that."

"Damn, I thought that was tomorrow night? Seriously, I love that you love those kids, but that's the fifth night in a row you're spending with them instead of me."

She smiled at him; he was easily disarmed. She pushed him back onto the bed, jumped on top of him, and leaned in slowly for a kiss, which he accepted.

"At least you have me every morning." She smiled, got off the bed, and resumed getting dressed.

As her perfectly formed dress dropped below her breasts, he glanced at the same belly button biology revealed on her abdomen.

No, we're not like other immigrants at all.

Chapter Two

KELLAN STOOD BESIDE Tendra in a large group of Travelers in front of an impressive screen in a common area aboard their ship. They were excited and anxious to see their leader and his exchange with the President of the United States of America. This was the moment that they had waited for; first for the twenty years leading up to their arrival, and then the additional four years of precautionary vetting before the first of them would be allowed off the ship.

The humans' first Asian-American president, John Umani, was about to speak on behalf of his people. His resting smile appeared sincere. He was dark-skinned, with even darker manicured hair and a confident stance. Kellan's friends and other Travelers talked about having faith in this president, but Kellan's father had taught him not to trust too easily, a precaution that all future leaders had to learn. They had spent the last four years following Umani's administration and their efforts to bring the Travelers to Earth. He was the human who would help them become citizens of the world—or so he said.

Not only was his father the first Traveler to leave the ship, to stand on Earth, but he would be standing side by side with the leader of the free world. This last fact, the inevitable handshake between the two, would be more than symbolic. Human and alien skin-to-skin contact, broadcast for the world to see. Travelers and human enthusiasts alike expected that it would be the precursor to their acceptance by the human race. If the president welcomed them, if he touched one of them without hesitation, then how could the rest of the world not accept them? This was their thinking, not Kellan's. He wasn't just skeptical, he was in awe of how easily everyone else trusted that this would all work out in their favor. Maybe he read and studied too much world history, but he just couldn't find many examples throughout humanity's time on Earth where they were so accommodating of foreigners. Why should the Travelers be different? Because they were hovering above this planet in their spaceship full of aliens?

Positioned under the Statue of Liberty, the humans' leader stood at a podium with dozens of cameras and microphones pointed in his direction. In the background, up in the sky, a morning moon was visible with a clear, reflective, metallic ball next to it. Their spaceship.

It was a long four years, for Kellan especially. When the alien ship was first detected and contact was made, the humans seemed to prepare for every worst case scenario. Governments around the world assembled their military and put on massive displays, showing off their troops, tanks, and missiles. The White House was barely recognizable behind a barricade of tanks and surface to air missile sentries. Other nations prepared in kind, with some going as far to set curfews and limit travel. Some religious leaders called for a rejection of

Kellan's kind, spouting out passages from Revelations, calling the Travelers the opening of the apocalypse. Kellan knew the Bible, they all did, and while he could see why they were concerned, there were other religious types who called for followers to praise the return of the gods from Greek and Roman mythology. Scholars began to consider the intellectual questions. Where did they come from, how did they get here, and why were they coming? Again, all of these questions were expected. All the Travelers knew how to address them if asked. They didn't know any more than humans. That was the response programmed into them. It was easy to remember because it was true.

Kellan had watched many debates from the ships' monitors, carried across the news networks, presenting the arguments for and the arguments against the benevolent, more enlightened, who would either come to usher in an age of peace or enslave the human race in perpetual servitude.

It was all ridiculous to him. So much speculation, but no one had yet met him and his kind at that point. It was all just wild guess work.

Within a year of their arrival, the military men and the ambassadors began showing up. Kellan had watched his father, Ringbak Arr, deal with delegation after delegation. The human delegations who were brought up to the ship over the course of the last three years were interested in biological testing, access to the ship's technology, and their enhanced security sessions where they interviewed the Travelers to determine the presence of a threat. Some of the ones who volunteered were his friends. He heard stories that the interviews went beyond questions and involved torture. No one ever talked about it or confirmed it, and Kellan never saw it first-hand, but he would see the uneasiness in his father's eyes, the blank stares that accompanied the non-answers Kellan would get when pressing for information. Over the course of four years, Kellan went from hopeful and optimistic to saddened and disillusioned by what he saw—distrustful men who came looking for reasons to say no to the Travelers coming down to Earth. Then there were the greedy humans who sought to exploit the Travelers' technology for their own profit and were using the threat of permanent exile in space as a motivator to get it. They came in suits but were flanked by soldiers. It was understood that these were the real leaders, the ones who bought the politicians and the policies of the world.

The way Kellan saw it, the Travelers' arrival came with a choice. Humanity had the option to accept the Travelers and welcome the great opportunity that they brought for growth and evolution, or they could cower behind their fears and let those fears dictate their future. Believing that the time for progress had arrived offered incredible opportunity to those who thought that they could learn from the aliens, but others saw it as a disruption of life as they knew it; they saw only the potential for colonization by an invading force. Kellan knew there would be those who didn't want them, but there would be plenty more who couldn't resist the idea that somehow they would benefit personally and financially from the Travelers, and because of that, they would be welcomed.

The gathered Travelers, all clothed in shiny, silver, and gold materials, watched a giant screen aboard their ship. These were their dress clothes. Tendra really knew how to work with the material, designing her own dresses all the time, and she really knew how to wear them, especially the gold. She wrapped the material tight around her body, showing herself off on purpose, but Kellan knew it was meant for him. He watched her; she was strikingly beautiful, and her smile lit up the room. A crowd always gathered around her when she entered the room; this time was no different. The second she smiled and showed her pristine teeth, they came, gathered around her, complimented her clothes, hugging, waiting for her to touch them ever so slightly on their shoulders, hands, or side. They showed the same enthusiasm for him, but he was their leader's son. *Perhaps it was formal, required,* he thought. He didn't care for the attention anyway, but he loved watching her in a crowd.

The Travelers looked like humans in every way. There was no discernible difference except that their clothes and their complexions were clean and lighter than seemed natural. Even those with dark skin had a lighter hue about them. Some in the media had likened it to the translucent skin of a jellyfish or glass frog, which Kellan found rather insulting. They weren't slimy amphibians, though he did think it'd be cool to electrocute someone with a mere touch like an eel. That ability would give him comfort when the military scientists came aboard his ship to do their "experiments."

Humanity is a fickle thing, he thought, watching the screen broadcast the empty stage where his father would soon stand. Society's ability to shift gears, to change direction and go from compassionate and tolerant to cruel and cold was as predictable as it was unpredictable. It would happen, these shifts, that much was certain, but when and how nobody knew, and no one could predict the future.

Kellan remembered how he, Tendra, and the rest of the Travelers waited for word from their leader at first contact. Education during the last few years of their travel focused almost entirely on the question, "How will we be received?"

Kellan and the others, in a sort of graduate level study, debated human history and how the current geo-political and socio-economic conditions might influence their reception. Kellan took the strong position that they would be received well at first due to their superior technology. No doubt they would be welcomed into the schools and homes of intellectuals everywhere who would be eager to learn what they knew. But that sentiment would shift when they learned there was very little new science to be gained. Tendra often countered his argument though and suggested that while she agreed the human fascination with her people would be short lived once they realized that most Travelers had a very limited understanding of the advanced technologies that brought them to Earth, they would begin to be view as equals, living at the whim of the universe and the men who lead the world, just like humans did.

Behind the stage was the Statue of Liberty. The American humans viewed their Statue of Liberty as a sign of freedom and acceptance, so it felt like as fitting a backdrop as any other. World leaders arrived and sat in their seats on the stage. Ringbak walked casually up the steps and also took his position.

President Umani took to the microphone. "Good morning, my fellow Americans, distinguished guests from across the globe, and all men, women, and children from around the world. It is with great pleasure and enthusiasm that I am here speaking to you today. From 1892 to 1954, over twelve million people have entered the United States through the portal of Ellis Island. They were immigrants in search of a better life, a new home, and a new community to be a part of. In the years since that time, we've been through a lot of ups and lot of downs. Together, as a country, we've seen many changes throughout every aspect of our great nation, and our world. Some of those changes have diminished us. For too long we've let our core values and the principles of our democracy fall too far behind because of self-interest. We were the leaders of what was once called the "free world," but not so much anymore. The time to change that story–our story–is upon us.

"Four years ago, we learned a truth about our world, our lives, and our universe. All the petty problems that we have, all the differences between each other and between different countries and all the countless years spent fighting each other no longer mattered. For we learned the most valuable and important truth to come out of the last thousand years. We learned that we are not alone."

Kellan grinned. He'd waited a long time for these words.

President Umani continued, "When the Traveler ship first appeared to us, we reacted from a place of fear. We instinctively thought to fight, but we didn't. We waited, we watched, and most of us trusted. Now, here we are all together on this stage in unity."

The president gestured toward rows of foreign leaders and dignitaries. Some exuded comfort and excitement through their smiles, while others sat with crossed arms and flaccid smiles, appearing to only be doing their duty.

"After four years of slowly getting to know our neighbors from beyond, and after inspecting them for any potential health risks, incompatibilities, and threats to humanity, the day has finally arrived where we have decided that it is time to open our minds, open our hearts, and open the doors of the free world, once again, to those who would seek to be a part of our society and our country. America was beautiful once. A dream built by those who knew what we could be. We've strayed from that in recent years. We've gone too far in establishing our dominance across the globe, and we've paid a heavy price. We can be better, we are better, and the Travelers have brought us an opportunity to be better. Soon, the Travelers will come down to our land, to our home, as our guests and as the product of the American immigration process. I am thrilled that we will be the first nation to welcome and host the Travelers to come live and work amongst us. As a renewed symbol of who we are, I am dedicating the new torch of Lady Liberty herself to our guests, the Travelers."

With a wave of his arm, the president signaled men at a switchboard down below. As trumpets blew a dazzling tune, massive, golden lights burst on and emanated from a newly designed torch atop the hand of the Statue of Liberty.

The Travelers rushed to the windows aboard their ship. As shipmates around him giggled and cheered,

Kellan forced a smile. The humans didn't know them. This planned exchange felt like a betrayal, leaving his hopes diminished. Umani's plastic smile was another reminder that the world they were about to enter was full of deceptive and cunning humans, each with their own agenda.

Umani continued in stride, "The Travelers bring a new future, no doubt full of wonder and questions. It is with that wonder that I welcome the first of the Travelers onto our land and up onto this stage to stand before you. Ladies and gentlemen, please join me in welcoming their leader, Ringbak Arr."

The crowd stood and applauded as Kellan's father approached the microphone. He was a tall, slender, but a fit man. On the stage Ringbak gave a warm, vibrant smile. At fifty years old, he looked like everyone else in the human audience, except a tad more confident, healthy, and strong in his stature. Behind his thinning, blond hair and squinted eyes was a man who Kellan didn't trust. Like the rest of the Travelers, Kellan relied on Ringbak to open the door to this new world and gain access to Earth, but as a leader he was distant and calculating, often refusing to reveal details and information with his people. Even to Kellan himself, and they were blood.

The fact that the Travelers shockingly did not know where they came from was accepted as unknown by all, except Kellan. A few days ago, he overheard his father arguing with another Traveler in his office. Kellan had never seen the other Traveler before, and the next day that Traveler went missing, then a few days later was found unconscious in the food holds. He was in a coma and was yet to come out of it. As strange as it was, no one questioned it. Kellan decided not to either. Still, he had no choice but to place his hope in his father. For now, he was their only option to secure their future, and he was the reason they were finally making it down to Earth.

In the lower corner of the screen, Kellan watched a group of protestors. Their loud chants temporarily drew the attention of the anchors. "We will not be colonized!" and "You will not replace us!" seemed to be the most popular phrases amongst them. Kellan had been watching them grow from the safety of his ship, but now his father was standing on the same ground as the ones sworn to oppose his arrival. These protests could grow and, Kellan feared, so could their power.

Ringbak looked beyond the crowd toward the protest noise but didn't break his charming smile. He spoke in a confident tone. "For their entire lives, my people and I have lived aboard a ship, never knowing of any world outside of its cold, metal walls. Every Traveler was born and raised on our ship, eventually realizing that we were on a journey toward Earth. There is a vast library on our ship, and all the tools were there for us to grow up. Every day we learned and studied about Earth and humanity, your history, your art, and your science. It is from our reading and learning about your history that my people knew we would be welcomed, just as millions have been welcomed here before us. It is also why this moment was not rushed.

"Four years have passed since we entered your orbit. That time was necessary for us to reveal ourselves and for your leaders to consider what our existence means."

Kellan wasn't sure what it meant anymore. They came here to be free and for a new life, but he was not so sure Earth was the place for that anymore. What did his ancestors see in this place to send them here? The crowd in front of Ringbak erupted with cheers and applause. Those seated in the small group looked happy to have these new members of society in their midst.

Tendra squeezed his hand, drawing his attention down to her at his side. Her expression was pure joy. He'd known her long enough, ten years now, to be able to tell when she was all in on something–this was one of those times. Kellan wanted her to be happy even if his own enthusiasm was waning, and he knew that she could also tell by his own expression what he was feeling.

"Don't be so nervous, Kel. This is a big moment, can't you just enjoy it?" Her question wasn't really a question at all.

Under the shadow of the Statue of Liberty, Ringbak Arr continued, "My people look very much the same as you, humans. We consider it a gift to us. All of the souls that I represent spent years looking in the mirror, wondering, guessing, and assuming why it is that we look like you. Are we human? How could that be, if we are? Were we from another Earth somewhere, heading home, perhaps? I could go on and on. The questions that we had about ourselves were endless, as I'm sure yours are as well. The truth is that we have no idea where we came from, as surprising as that is, or why we look just like you. Over the last four years we've worked with the international science community to provide the answers to as many of these questions as we could. In the process, and thanks to all those dedicated, and excited–," he said with a wink and a smile, "–scientists, we actually learned something about ourselves, and inadvertently we learned something about all of you as well–something astounding."

Kellan watched as those on the ship inched closer to the screen. Their whispers filled the air, bodies shifted, and heads turned toward each other. They were all curious, including Tendra.

"What answers, Kellan? What is he talking about? Does he know where we came from?"

"I don't know," Kellan said.

President Umani stepped forward. "Ringbak and the rest of the Traveler Nation have no knowledge from the time before they were born on their ship. They don't possess any information about their origins or even their technology. In fact, they have as much to learn about how they got here as we do. We've been through every section of the ship, investigated every aspect of their tech, and interviewed hundreds of the Travelers."

Kellan huffed. Interviews? In the deepest of the night, screams coming from the Emigrati could be heard throughout the halls. Emigrati were the volunteers, like his friends, those who were eager to prove to the world that they did not mean any harm. It worked, but it never sat right with Kellan. What type of people could comfortably give tests that tortured others? Was that a place where they wanted to live?

He would never let them do that to Tendra.

Back at the podium, Ringbak stepped back toward the microphone. "For the first time, we have an understanding of why we are here. We are alien, we know this by our DNA. It's been studied and unpacked, and it simply does not exist anywhere on Earth–part of it anyway, most of it. But some of our makeup, some of our DNA and genetic coding is, well ... it is human. We are hybrids of a sort, a mixture of you and our ancestors from wherever we came from, but that is only part of the story."

Of course. It all makes sense now. Their ancestors must have known somehow. That a part of them was human only cements that they did, in fact, belong on Earth, that's why they were here. Kellan found comfort in this answer, which while small, was incredibly significant.

"The most fascinating aspect is that each and every one of us Travelers are linked to people here on Earth: a mother, a grandmother, great-great-grandmother, brother, sister, or father. We are your children, myself included, and some of you are our parents."

Rows and rows of Kellan's fellow Travelers were overcome with varying emotions of happiness, confusion, surprise, and overwhelm. This news was everything to them, it was everything to Kellan in a way, as he never felt he really belonged here. But it was Tendra who was on her knees, hands to her face, bawling, crying, laughing. Kellan joined her on the floor. They hugged. He knew how much this meant to her. She never knew her parents, few of them did. The way in which they came into their world was wrought with issues, pain, and death. Maybe she could find family here; for the first time she could have that.

"I know this is confusing and unbelievable to many. How is this possible, you must want to know. This is mostly a mystery to us as well, but from what we can gather, for decades, all across the Earth humans have reported strange lights in the night sky, mysterious visions of alien beings in their bedrooms, and some have vivid memories of being on spaceships, seeing themselves pregnant and meeting their own alien-human hybrid child only to awake with a sense of loss and confusion, and no child. There have been reports of disappearances into powerful lights, foreign object implants, and stories so wild that, until four years ago, would garner ridicule and scorn. But some of those stories must now be considered true. While it wasn't us, there must have been others, our predecessors, our ancestors, who have been working for decades to bring us together. Since we don't understand the technology that created us or even brought us here, we also don't know *how* this is possible, just that it is. Clearly there is much more to learn, but we are the product of what we believe to be a genesis of the best of two kinds of species. There is more though. Through this incredible partnership and alliance between my kind and yours, we were able to accomplish something extraordinary. We possess a list of relations to you that will be released and entrusted to your governments. We know who you are related to, and we plan to reunite you with the ones that you've never met. Your children, grandchildren, your great-great-grandchildren, brothers, and sisters."

Kellan could see that while all eyes were on Ringbak, something else was afoot on the stage. The president had advisors energetically rambling in his ear. They continually looked off into the distance as the protestors' chants grew louder, their battle cry growing.

"Did you know this, Kellan?" Tendra looked up at him with round eyes. "Is it true?"

Kellan shook his head slowly, not knowing what to think. "I'm not sure I understand. I don't ... know. My father never said anything to me."

Kellan's curiosity for the scene on the stage was eclipsed by the feelings of betrayal. Why was he unworthy of his father's trust? He drew himself closer to Tendra and held her tight while he looked back up to the screen. He attempted to put his thoughts to words. "He's saying that we are part human. How long has he known? Why didn't he tell me?"

"We have family on Earth?" Tendra whispered in awe. "How is this possible?"

He felt the weight of numerous eyes on him and glanced up, meeting the gazes of his people looking to him for more answers. After all, he was the leader's son. If only he did know.

But his thoughts, and probably the thoughts of everyone else on the ship, were suddenly rocked by the sounds and images of multiple explosions off the island, in the distance, in Manhattan.

He shot to his feet and grabbed Tendra's wrist, pulling her as he raced from the room. "Come on, we need to get out of here."

Chapter Three

THE LONG, BRIGHT hallway along the outer end of the Travelers' spaceship had been primarily used for moving large pallets of goods from the food storage holds. Right now, it was helping Kellan find the most direct path to his father. He moved fast, too fast for Tendra.

"Kellan, slow down!" she demanded before stopping herself.

"Sorry, I need to see him, don't you want to know what's going on?"

"Yes, but his ship just returned, they're not going to let you in right away, you know that!" She was right. There was a strict protocol Ringbak had to follow whenever he returned. Ensuring that he didn't bring any foreign bacteria back with him, checking his vitals, his blood, and a host of other procedures. Still, Kellan wanted to be there the moment he would be allowed in.

"I'm going, are you coming with me or not?" he asked.

"I'm not," she said in her steadfast, arms crossed, unmovable way.

"Fine," he replied before turning away from her and storming off down the hallway.

Being the son of Ringbak Arr had granted Kellan more access to what was unfolding than perhaps a young Traveler should have had, but not this, the most important information. Nevertheless, he'd learned more in the last four years than he had in the last twenty. While the humans were poking and prodding his kind and his home, he had a front row seat to what he thought was all the secrets their ship held. That is until his father dropped the bomb about their lineage, a reminder that his father still kept many things from him. Still, Kellan learned the truths about humanity, or at least those aspects presented before him.

When NASA first learned about the Traveler ship, four years ago, they were keen to get their hands on it, that was made clear by the initial but unnecessary threat that came first from the ground. That access was quickly granted. While most intellectuals and scientists wanted desperately to gain a peek inside, there was a small group who wanted more than anything to get a close look at the outside, taking interest in the ship's mechanical structure. The ship was shaped like an egg, with more defined curves and a clear lead point. In the rear, there was what looked like an antenna jutting out pointedly.

Though the ship was massive, it was thought that ninety percent of the interior was used for housing the one hundred thousand Travelers. Kellan hated being called that. Travelers, to him, equated to conquerors, as they knew Earth's history with "travelers." They did not want to be seen as colonizing anything; rather, they saw themselves as migrants aboard a boat, searching for a final resting spot, that is why they call themselves, "Travelers." They got along with it anyway; it seemed to make their presence more understandable to humans, and besides, it had been adopted by the media around the globe already and there was no changing that. Now, some called them Travs, some kind of slur meant to make them feel dirty, less than, whatever. The humans that hated them or distrusted them even named the ship Ithaca, a misplaced reference to the Trojan Horse.

The term Travs made no sense; they were far from dirty. The inside of the ship was clean, really clean, it was mostly white and was accented by a luminous red, runner light that moved throughout the curved hallways and travel corridors, sometimes on the walls or ceiling. It was presumed to be a guiding light of sorts, one that helped those who needed direction. Although clean and pristine, it was not an artificial or cold environment; instead, it was more contemporary than minimalist. There were plush and comfortable quarters of ample size. There were condos for the younger and unburdened. And for those with their own children there were communities of homes that resembled earthly abodes in mini suburban-city environments. These family homes encircled a grassy park the size of a football field, and when you looked up you saw bright blue sky with a perfect arrangement of carefully placed cumulous clouds. Kellan didn't grow up in one though. His living accommodations were more like a penthouse apartment or the residence of the white house. There was no grassy field to run around on, there was no catch being played with his father.

Being the son of the leader, he was kept busy in formal environments like offices, meeting rooms, and the like. Kellan never knew his mother, she had died during childbirth, something he did share with the other children his age and the one deadly aspect of life on the ship. Many of the mothers of the first kids, the ones born at the start of the journey, died during childbirth. Then there were the suicides. When Kellan was very young, between four and six years old, many of the men, ages twenty-five to forty, took their own lives. As he grew up and entered adolescence, Kellan hoped he'd get off the ship before he reached twenty-five, just in case it had to do with age, like a disease. That was really the only reason to leave, that and because Tendra wanted him to, and the responsibility, of course. He was still holding out hope that he wouldn't have to take his father's place, but it was expected that he would.

The non-housing parts of the ship were for congregating, eating, education, research and science, life support that was carried out automatically by the ship itself, and of course propulsion.

Propulsion was perhaps the biggest mystery, both to the humans and to the Travelers. Since the Travelers were being prepared for life on Earth within the confines of human technology, they were never given access to the propulsion or any advanced navigation systems. They monitored the ship's course in a rudimentary way, sort of a "space travels for beginners" level. The whole time though, throughout all of their lives, the ship had been traveling at what appeared to be the speed of light, some sort of warp speed until it stopped just three hundred million miles from Earth. They still had no idea how it was possible or even what the drive system was made of.

So, their arrival to Earth was never really a choice. Nothing in Kellan's live was, so it seemed.

Kellan rushed down the hall toward the infirmary where his father would first be taken for his vitals check. He glared over his shoulder at that red light that chased behind him on the floor–it seemed so random, who it followed, who it guided. There were attempts made to learn about the propulsion system over the years, as evidenced by the blast markings and scratches on the sealed walls that lead to "the hum," the sound that was believed to come from the engine, but no one ever penetrated the wall. Whenever they tried, that red light was there, streaking about overhead, as if it was watching them. The red light followed all of them at some point. He never knew its significance. He assumed it was a monitor of some sort, like security to keep them out of the propulsion room. But if that was the case, then who programmed it? Maybe it was the first ones like Kellan's grandfather, Mancie Arr, whose only mission seemed to have been the procreation of a son and grandson, and who died at ninety-one years of age. Mancie Arr was the first leader of the Travelers, and his origin story was fuzzy to say the least. Mancie claims to have awoken on the ship, mid-flight, with his sweetheart lying next to him, hand in hand.

When he composed himself, he found that there were others aboard, already hard at work, moving about, setting things up and moving things in. They helped settle him in, calmed him down, and explained to him that he was part of a scientific mission and both he and his fiancé had fallen and suffered minor amnesia. They showed him the inner workings of the ship, which he didn't recognize, of course, while his fiancé, Bel-an, was taken to their quarters. After a long and exhaustive instructional period that the workers claimed would help restart his memory, he retired to his quarters, where he found a captain's uniform, the same one that Ringbak wore today.

When he woke up the next morning, Mancie went looking for those who instructed him and he found them missing, all of them gone, and in their place were tens of thousands of new faces, all gathered at the center park. Not one of them had any memory of where they had been prior. Just like Mancie, they all simply "awoke" there.

The problem with Mancie's story was that neither he nor any of the others who were considered to be the "first ones" were around to support any of what he said. They had all since passed, and what remained was nothing more than the rumor, gossip, and oral recounting of how they all came to be aboard the ship.

One thing was clear amongst Kellan's generation, though: no one believed it.

To them it was as simple as asking, *Why wouldn't the "first ones" write down their story? Why is there no record of it anywhere?* And that was the issue. There was no record of the origins of neither the ship nor its inhabitants anywhere to be found. This one, uncomfortable fact was the only thing that could divide them. This was their only Achilles' heel, and Kellan knew it and he was sure that his father did too.

Every day Travelers walked past each other, nodding and saying hello. Men and women looked over important papers and tablets as they walked. Absent were the droids in place of pets that would normally accompany the halls of a spaceship from movies and television. Instead there were plants everywhere. The lush green was in stark contrast to the bright white everything. Plants were placed every ten feet on both sides of the hallway that Kellan rushed through. There even seemed to be pleasurable conversations happening around them. Kellan wondered at the foolishness of men who debated philosophy of leaves. He thought those conversations luxuries, distractions from their task, whatever it might be. This had been his home for his whole life, everything that he knew was here, but now after the DNA revelation, he, like the rest of the Travelers suspected there were more secrets to be uncovered.

Kellan arrived at the private medical partition where he found two large unarmed guards, Euro and Marz. The guards raised a hand to stop Kellan, barring him from entrance with a simple gesture. His needs would have to wait. He always had to wait.

Still, he was concerned and declared as much. "I have a right to see my father."

The guards shook their heads.

"You know how it goes, Kellan," Euro said. "You'll be permitted in once the doctors have finished."

Kellan clenched his hands at his sides. He relented to pacing the hall outside the partition, awaiting permission to see his father. As his pacing picked up, his anger grew. He was angry over the secrets, covert meetings, deals, and plans—the things that had been happening for years.

He was angry at his father but also at himself. How could he miss it, all of it—the connection to earthlings, the now-clear danger of going down to the planet? Would they all be targeted, the Travelers, him, Tendra? Would they even get the chance to find their human family or would they be stopped before they could even try? The explosions were so far from the stage that they couldn't have been meant for his father, but who were they meant for? The protestors of the protestors? The ones who wanted to welcome the Travelers, apparently.

Rumors had floated around the ship for all of Kellan's life that they could be human, given their looks and the ship's programmed destination. Maybe that really upset some of the humans. Not even the eldest amongst them had answers though, as they were born or "awakened" on the ship with no memory of the time before. It was thought they were fleeing a dying planet and heading back home to Earth, but after seeing how advanced their technology was compared to the scientists who came aboard from Earth, Kellan doubted that human origin was ever a real possibility.

Tired of waiting, Kellan turned to the sentry standing outside the door. "How long is this doctor going to take? Answer me, or I swear I'll punch your expressionless face."

Euro's eyes narrowed. "I want answers too, Kellan. I want to know what we are. We all do."

Kellan's hands relaxed as his anger disappeared and shame replaced it. Everyone was confused, and he was the only one with access to the information that they all wanted. He was to be their leader one day. The questions that he wanted answered weren't only for him, they were for everyone. The attendant was a brother in all of this, not an enemy.

"I'm sorry. He's our leader–your leader–and he is the strongest amongst us. I will find out what is going on and I will tell everyone, I swear it." Kellan saw the look in the attendant's eyes, the fear eclipsed by a moment of hope, but Kellan knew no such hope, for he knew his own father. He knew an answer was the last thing that he'd get.

The High Security Detail, adorned with the crispest and darkest clothing of anyone on the ship, advanced toward Kellan's. The HSD formed eight years ago when they first arrived in this corner of the galaxy and began making plans for contact with humanity. They were highly-skilled and lethal. Kellan's father decided that on this new world he'd no doubt need protection and went to great lengths to prepare, but for his first trip to Earth, he wasn't allowed his own security.

They were interrupted by the sudden opening of the vacuum sealed door and the pouring out of nearly a dozen doctors and nurses. "Kellan, you can see your father now," Euro indicated to Kellan with a swift gesture toward the door. As Kellan passed, Euro sent him a hopeful but scared glance, as if to say, "help us."

Kellan entered and stood at the entrance while his father got off the bed and started to get dressed. "Everything okay?"

"Yes, son, I'm fine, as always." Something Kellan had a hard time believing while surveying the countless tubes, monitors, drips, and other odd machines. Ringbak caught Kellan's drifting glare.

Ringbak reached out and placed his hands over Kellan's. Kellan felt them but where comfort and concern should lie, coldness and distance emerged.

These hands were not from father to son but from boss to employee.

"Father," Kellan spoke gruffly, " I need–"

"You need?" Ringbak scoffed, releasing Kellan from his grip. "A leader doesn't focus on his needs. Have you learned nothing about ego and self-importance?"

"I am sorry, Father." Kellan bowed his head. "Our people are scared and confused. They need to know more about your statement that we're part human with relations here on Earth, that our people have family here, that we're somehow tied to someone on Earth, is ..."

"Confusing," Ringbak offered.

Kellan glowered at him. "Dammit, Father, why didn't you tell me? Do I have people here? On Earth? Who are they, what do they know, how did this happen? What about all the parents of the children aboard our ship? Am I your son or am I not?!"

Ringbak coughed into his hand. The raspy wetness of it worried Kellan that his dad was lying to him yet again.

Doctors, who must have been waiting outside, moved in.

Ringbak's breaths wheezed out of him as he struggled to stay composed. "I know it doesn't make sense right now, but it will, give me time. I will address everything that is known about our origins, our DNA, and our relations on this planet soon enough. You will take your place among your relations on Earth and with patience, you will meet your human mother."

The instruments beeped erratically. The doctors covered Ringbak in a fury of medical attention, and Kellan was ushered out.

"What's wrong? Are you sick? What's happening?"

"I'll be fine. These re-entries into space just take their toll, that's all."

But something was off. Kellan had seen this process a dozen times so far, all of his father's secret off ship meetings with the leaders of Earth and all the human visitors they'd endured, none of those times did they use this equipment.

"What is that device?" He demanded, pointing to the hand-held scanner that beeped like a Geiger counter, but before he could be answered, he was pushed out by the HSD.

Kellen left and stormed down the pristine and serene hallway. He had a mother. How could this be? More lies and things his father had kept from him. He clenched his fists and ground his teeth; those around him stayed out of his way. Dismissal from his father agitated him even more. None of it made sense–how was it possible? Kellan thought about the timeline; his mother would have needed to have him around twenty years ago? But they'd been on the ship since then; the timeline, it made no sense to him. They had never been to Earth. How could he have a human mother? When and where would his father have met her?

He was so enraged that he ran right past Tendra who was walking toward the medical area.

"Kellan, stop! Where are you going?!"

"Tendra?"

He turned to her, half-charging down the hall toward the only one he trusted. She held out her arms and he saw her eyes, her tears, and the force of her sadness and pain stopped him dead.

"What's wrong?" she pleaded.

"I have a mother, Tendra, and my father knows where she is." His voice sounded more controlled than he felt.

"How is that even possible?"

"I don't know!" he yelled.

Her eyes went wide. Then, slowly, she reached up and touched him. First on his cheek, then she took his hands and wrapped her tiny fingers around them.

His rage faded and with a deep breath he blew the last of it out.

Kellan looked down at the love of his life. "We deserve answers, and we deserve to know what is going on, and I will find out who did this to him, but it's not right what he did."

Tendra squeezed his hands and then she led him over to a bench, a quiet space around the corner, and away from the main thoroughfare.

Looking deep into his eyes, she smiled, disarming him. "Kellan, my love, we were born and raised on a ship, alone in the middle of space, headed for Earth. That's pretty crazy when you think about it. There's still so much we don't know about ourselves–who we are, where we came from, and why we are here. I'm sure there will be things that we'll love to hear and other things, like this, that we won't. But good or bad, we will always have each other to go through it with."

The world drowned out around them. He was overcome with love, gratitude, and happiness in that very moment.

"When did you become the sensible one?" He smiled down at her. "Tendra, I'm not sure what will happen to us on Earth after seeing what they did to my father. Maybe we should be concerned."

Kellan took a moment to consider what he was about to say. "I think there's more going on with the humans than we've been told. My father is not himself."

Tendra placed her hands on her hips. "Of course he isn't, he just told you about your mother."

Kellan wasn't so sure. "No, it's not just that. There's something else he's hiding. All these lies, the things that he's known for a while and never shared. What else does he know, what else isn't he telling us?"

Kellan intended on finding the answer.

"Kellan, take a breath, wait it out. Give your father a few days, wait and see what he says when he addresses us."

Kellan stared out the window at the stars and that damn bright, blue ball that floated in space below them.

Chapter Four

TIMESTAMP: UNKNOWN
LOCATION: RESERVED GYM

KELLAN TRAINED EVERY day. As the son of the leader, he had to be strong. To never be a target for those who might seek to kidnap and use him as leverage over his father. Weakness was not part of the plan for his new life. But today, he needed the training to control his rage. His blood was still boiling from the interaction with his father. One thing that always worked after their so many confrontations and arguments was a good workout.

Ropes, weights, sticks, and blades lined the walls of the gym. Kellan always thought it odd that they could train with blades, yet they were forced to walk the ship unarmed. As he grew, he thought less about why they were available to him as he did about how to use them. The speckles of dried blood peppered throughout the white room served as a sign of their use, and a warning that others were already training with the assortment of short daggers.

Whose blood was it, he wondered every time he came in. He thought about that blood too often.

It even looked like human blood.

This gym was his private room, no one else had access to it. Besides, there were dozens of fantastic gym rooms across the ship, one for every sector.

But today was different. Today he had a partner.

"Why don't you just ask your father?" Tendra posed as she bounced into ready position, arms raised, gloves up, ready for a fight.

"I tried that already," he ground out.

Her stare was hypnotic, distractingly so, almost intoxicating. Her eyes were like something from a dream, a fantasy, so bright, so green and blue, like the waves miles below them. Hypnotic, yes, intoxicating yes, dangerous ... definitely. That was one of the things that he liked about her. That and the way her body looked in skin tight training pants. Her curves made him want to reach out and hold onto her every chance he could. Her lips, so plump, so perfect, if she'd just allow it, he'd lock onto them and never let go. He was so in love with her.

Tendra punched him in the nose, sending Kellan back a few steps, stunned. "What the hell, Ten!"

"Pay attention!" She scowled at him. "You're a million miles away. What if you asked your father's guard to look into it? He follows your father everywhere, he has to know or have seen something."

"And what makes you think he'd tell me? His loyalty is to my father, and he's not exactly at the top of my trust list." He raised his fists and got into stance. "Can we just spar?"

"I still think it's a worth a try."

He sighed. "Fine, I'll ask him, but I doubt it'll do any good." He nodded to her. "Now, hands up. You got a hit off me, but don't think I'll make it that easy on you again. I want you to be ready for whatever we encounter down there."

Kellan removed his gloves and so did Tendra.

"Now, take this knife," Kellan insisted, forcing the dagger into her hand. "It's a four-part move, remember? Evade my attack, drop, then slice my leg, then throw it at the attacker."

"Kellan, I don't like this." She frowned and stiffened. "I already have the punching and kicking down that you taught me, I don't want to use a knife."

"I know, but look, I'll always do everything in my power to protect you, but you'll still need to know how to defend yourself in a more damaging way. There will be times when punching and kicking won't be enough. My father says that we are fools if we do not use that which we are given, regardless of if we know exactly why we were given it. Now, get ready."

Kellan took a step back and raised his fists and lurched forward only to be met with the equal and opposing force of Tendra's foot to his groin. Kellan dropped to his knees and groaned. "Tendra what the..."

She raised her chin. "See, a kick can be enough."

"Point made." He glowered up at her. "Now, help me up."

She took his hand and helped pull him to his feet. She shifted, and her brows pinched. "I'm sorry. I told you I didn't want to do this."

She tossed the knife to the ground beside Kellan and raced out beyond the auto-doors, disappearing into the busy halls of the ship.

Kellan glanced down at the knife on the white

floor next to those minuscule blood dots. That could just as easily be Tendra's blood. He couldn't bear the thought of someone hurting her. The threats weren't only going to come from the outside. Tendra was his reason to be strong, but she was also his weakness. Would his father use her against him, if he saw fit? He removed his gloves and picked up the blades from the ground where Tendra dropped them. One by one, he fired the weapons off into the practice dummy across the room, then turned toward the punching bag and lay into it, punching away until his knuckles became raw and bloody.

Kellan continued his workout with the daggers, holding two at a time, striking his home-made, stuffed victim one blow after another. It must have been three hours that went by. He didn't even notice and wouldn't have, but when the training doors opened and Tendra walked back in, he got a look at the clock. He also caught himself in the mirror. He was shirtless, sweaty, and buff, this was how he liked to see himself. Fit and dangerous.

He stopped when Tendra entered and smirked. Her fire-red hair was pulled back into a ponytail, her slender frame made more apparent by the extra skin tight workout pants and even tighter tank top. Her crystallized eyes were bright and held just a hint of mischief as she strode toward him.

"What? You look like you've never seen me like this before. You're right. Let's do this."

"I'm just ... glad to see that you're prepared for a real workout." He waggled his brows.

"Oh, this is the real one? I thought I won the last one when you dropped to the floor?"

"Cheap shot."

"If you say so. Where do you want me?" she asks with a devious grin.

"Grab your knives." He knew this would make her uncomfortable.

"Kellan, stop. Don't do this again. I promise I will let you teach me some things, but not the knives."

"That's exactly why I want you to pick them up. If you were as comfortable with a blade as you are with your hand-to-hand then I'd say we should try something else."

She reluctantly accepted one of the knives he held out for her.

"Why is it so important to you that I learn how to stab someone?" She gripped the handle loosely and unsure.

"It's not for stabbing, it's for throwing or slicing. We've been through this. I don't know what we'll expect down there. I may not always be there to protect you, and I want you to be able to defend yourself."

She nodded and looked at the knife in her hand. "I can't imagine we're going to a world where we need these, but okay, I'll give it a try."

Suddenly he charged, grabbing the knife from her hand and twisting her around so that he wound up behind her. He kept a firm grip on her, but not hard enough to hurt her. She struggled to break free, still holding the blade, but hesitant to threaten him with it.

"You can't hesitate, Ten. You have to move fast!"

"I don't like this. I'll do it, but I don't like it. I don't want to fight anyone."

"That's why we can't go down. You're not prepared, you won't prepare, and I'm not going to take you down until you are!"

"Imagine I'm a human, taking you away from me. I'm too big and too strong for you to fight hand-to-hand and win. But you have a knife, now use it against me!"

Instead, she cocked her head back, landing against his nose. His grip slipped, and she slid out from under him.

She swiveled around on him. "I told you, Kellan, I don't like knives, and I don't want to do this anymore, this was a bad idea!"

"What the hell, Tendra?" he yelled as he clutched his face. "What was that for?"

"You won't take me down? I want to go down with you, but don't think for a second that I can't go down on my own if you put me up against it!"

"Ten ..."

"No! You listen to me this time! I love you, I want to be with you, and that's not easy considering who you are. But you promised when we first started dating that you weren't going to be like this, that you were going to be your own man, not a fall-in-line diplomat's son! You promised!"

"Ten, I know but I, I don't want ..."

She rose, kicking him aside, and stormed out, once again leaving Kellan to stare at the white training floor.

He stood, furiously throwing the dagger that Tendra left behind. It landed square in the chest of the makeshift training dummy.

Chapter Five

KELLAN HIT THE buzzer button outside the entrance to the nursery aboard the ship. The look-through glass revealed a rumpus room full of kids between four and six, and behind that another room held the babies, the newborns. Tendra loved it in there, Kellan knew it gave her so much joy to be around children, but he felt jealous whenever he saw her with them.

An older woman opened the door and let him in. "Good evening, Kellan."

"Hello, Margerotta. Can I see Tendra?"

"Of course," the woman said, gesturing toward the newborn room.

Kellan made his way through the rumpus room. He'd been there so many times that these kids knew him and always ran to him when he came through.

"Kellan!" they all seemed to yell in unison.

"Hi Max, hello Clara, hi Ben, hi Quinta." He always rushed through though, pushing his way into Tendra's space, shutting the door behind him. She didn't turn though, just kept standing with her back to him while gently burping a baby.

"Ten, how long are you going to be like this for? I

mean, it's been almost a week already, come on," he pleaded, but nothing.

"I've said sorry, what else do you want from me?"

Tendra heard that and spun around. Her eyes were fierce but her lips demanded softly, "You know exactly what I want."

"Ten."

"No. I don't want to hear anything else from you except, 'okay, we can go down.'"

"Ten ..."

"Nope," she said before putting the baby down and walking past him into the rumpus room. She'd done this before when they were arguing. She knew he wouldn't get angry in front of the kids.

"Benjamin Raptor Rufus Wellington the third! How are you today?" she enthusiastically asked the six-year-old boy.

"You know that's not my real name!" He seemed to like this game.

"Oh, Miss Sabrina Everlasting, you are gracing the kingdom with her majesty's presence today even though thoust age is nine?"

Sabrina also liked this game, "Yes, Miss Tendra, I have come to invite my subject to the royal ball. You and you butler are also invited." She looked toward Kellan.

"Butler? I'm not her butler. I am her Majesty's royal guard!" He took a quick stance next to the girl. "Ready to fight off any invading forces and project thy kingdom!"

They were having fun, but Tendra didn't let Kellan join in for too long. "Unfortunately, your majesty must allow me to remove your royal guard as he's disturbing the villagers."

"What?" Kellan knew what she was up to.

"I understand. Guard, leave us."

"But ..." Kellan protested.

"I said leave us, guard!" Sabrina and Tendra laughed and Kellan reluctantly walked away. This would clearly have to wait until later.

When later came, he went looking for Tendra again. This time the hallways of the Travelers' ship were active, moving, bustling with excitement, energy, and enthusiasm.

"I'm all set for New Mexico tomorrow!"

"We're landing in Maine, and it's snowing there!"

"This time on Thursday I'll be dipping my toes in the Atlantic Ocean, if you can believe that."

Kellan couldn't move past the conversations fast enough. As hard as he tried, he couldn't escape the excitement. Kellan bumped into someone, sending the Traveler stumbling.

"Kel, hey." His friend, Aldum grinned. "Where are you going so fast? Are you heading down today?"

"No, just looking for Tendra. Have you seen her?"

His brows rose. "Hey, is it true that you can't leave? I mean, you'd tell me, right? Because some of the others are saying that you've got to work with your father on, you know, diplomatic stuff."

Two men sidled up by Aldum and sneered at Kellan. He didn't recognize them. They must have been from other sections. He was sure they saw the sweat on his forehead.

"Nah, he'll get to do whatever he wants, go wherever he wants I'm sure. Miami Beach I bet, or the Hamptons maybe?" the one on the right guessed. "Somewhere elite, for sure."

"Hey, maybe it's Nantucket or the Main Line?" The guy on the left nudged his friend, and they laughed.

Kellan bit back a groan of frustration. He didn't have time for this nonsense. He knew a rise was what they wanted. It's what they all wanted, the leader's son to lose his cool. What a story it would be to bring down to Earth and to their host families. "Have any of you seen Tendra today?"

He had been looking for her everywhere, starting with the nursery and the playroom. There were so many Traveler children born without parents, left to be raised by anyone who would. Tendra would have loved to take any of them in, she couldn't wait to be a mother. She was a natural with the children, and they all loved her. But she, like many of them, were too young to qualify for parental responsibility. She was nineteen and the rule was at least twenty-three. So she just spent as much of her free time as she could there, playing with the kids, doing puzzles and building forts. She'd hold and rock the newborn babies for hours, singing human lullabies to them as they drifted in and out of sleep. But she wasn't there today.

"I saw her and some girls headed into Cafeteria 9," the one on the left told him. "Why don't you just call her?"

"Thanks," he said and turned, hurrying down the hall. Of course he could call her, but he didn't want this conversation to be overheard. He only got a few more steps though.

"Kellan, stop," a familiar voice ordered.

Kellan halted and glared at Callum, his father's guard. His dark coat reflected off of the glimmering surroundings of the hallway, bathing them both in a red glow. Kellan didn't have time for him.

"Yes, Callum, what is it?"

"Your father would like to see you. He's been trying to reach you." Callum glanced at Kellan's wrist-com, which he quickly covered with his sleeve before meeting the guard's persistent gaze.

"You can let him know that I'll be there shortly," he snapped back before turning and walking away from them.

Callum's lips thinned. He was probably not used to being disobeyed or challenged. "STOP!" he shouted, forcing Kellan to stiffen up. He noticed that others stopped as well and were prepared for a show.

"Kellan, he wants you to come now. I will escort you, though I'd prefer not to."

"Can he wait five minutes for me to dip into the cafeteria to wish my girlfriend a happy anniversary?"

Callum's gaze moved past him. "Anniversary? You and Tendra aren't married."

"Anniversary of when we first picked out what our Earth pet will be. Mine will be a dog, a puppy, a Red Golden and she wants two cats, Main Coon. Typical. It's stupid, I know but you know how girls are."

Callum's brow furrowed. Yeah, he wasn't buying it.

"I'll just be five minutes then I'll come straight to him."

Callum glanced over Kellan's shoulder then met his gaze. "Okay, Kel, just don't get me in trouble with your dad. Please." That's how it was, and always had been. These guys had a job to do, they didn't want to get in trouble, busted down a rank over something like this, but they liked Kellan, they all did. He grew up with these guys, he'd sneak out to play with Aldum when they were teens. They always let him get away with whatever it was.

"Right. Be back in five, promise."

Kellan moved through the crowded cafeteria, quickly maneuvering around white circular tables, four to six Travelers per bench, facing another row of equally cramped young, enthusiastic migrant hopefuls.

He spotted Tendra across the room.

This wasn't where you went to get the best food on the ship but it was where you'd go to see friends, listen to music, and be loud without issue. It was a fun zone of sorts. Kellan and Tendra were used to a little more refinement though, like what Cafe 23 and Cafe 4 had to offer. Meticulously designed with gold accents, artwork, and polished silverware, they were reserved for High Counsel or High Authority members only. He remembered the first time he took Tendra to Cafe 4; she was so out of her element, not used to being served. In the general population food halls, they'd have to wait in line, and while the food was good, it was a cafeteria, not a restaurant. But it was free. He knew she preferred these food halls even though she had privileges at the nicer ones. She liked to be around regular people after all.

Kellan saw her interacting with them. He allowed himself a moment and watched her in her element. She was a soft girl when she wanted to be but a hard ass when necessary. He liked her like this. It made him smile, and he knew this could be the last time he saw her like this, standing among their own.

His wrist-com vibrated, pulling his attention away; it was his father again. He silenced the call and kept moving toward Tendra.

As he drew near, he heard more of the excitement, the key phrases above the chatter. New York, Miami, Chicago. Driving a car, hiking, swimming in the ocean. These were the same things he'd heard Travelers talk about for years, many years. Whenever he heard this kind of talk, all he could think about was genocide, Nazis, apartheid, border walls, invaders. Kellan was almost an expert in human history. His father demanded it, making him study the same histories over and over until he could recite the stories verbatim.

He'd prefer a blissful ignorance, never having read one page of human history. Then maybe he could share in the enthusiasm he saw, the laughter and friendships displayed with playful slapping of high fives and innocent jabs from one to another. Instead, he was bitter, resentful, and ashamed that they didn't know what was coming, what was really waiting for them down there.

They were fools. Most wouldn't fare well on Earth. He'd rather see them all off with a pat on the back and then take this ship for a spin around the stars, if he could. Maybe one day he'd figure out how. Tendra was at a table of her friends when Kellan's eyes finally rested on her position. Technically, they were his friends as well, but today they might as well be strangers because of their enthusiasm which he didn't share. They were eager and happy to see him as he stood tall above their table.

"Hey, Kellan! Can you believe it?" Erican said.

"Today is the day!" Relina grinned at him.

"I'm on the twenty-second ship down, later this week!" Froin chirped.

He ignored them all, shooting Tendra a look. Her brows pinched, and she looked away.

"Ten, I need to talk to you," he told her. She folded her arms, still not looking at him. He knew she'd still be mad about what happened in the gym, how he didn't want to leave the ship. He growled with impatience. "Ten, let's go down to Earth."

Tendra spun around and jumped to her feet, bouncing into Kellan's arms.

"Really, you mean it? You changed your mind? We can go?" Her excitement was one of the only things that made him feel good, but his body language revealed his nervousness.

"I mean it, we can go," he said as he scanned the room.

Tendra backed off, crossing her arms, narrowing her eyes, and turning her back. "Maybe I don't want to go now."

Must she be so difficult? He scowled at her. "Seriously? You're the one who wanted to go!"

"Not like this, Kellan. I want it to be fun. I want it to be marked as a happy memory, but you're not happy about it. I don't want this to be how we remember this moment."

"I want to build a life with you on Earth. I'm in, Ten, all in, one hundred percent. Just tell me what I can do."

"Then take me to Manhattan."

"Ten ..."

She raised her chin. "You asked what I want, well that's what I want. I want to go to New York and see Broadway, maybe even work there. I know you can make that happen, what with your big, strong, manly resources." She chuckled, squeezing his arm.

Protestors just bombed Traveler supporters during his father's speech, and she wanted to live there? Was she insane? Surely, there were other theaters in the world that she could go to.

"New York is dangerous." He brushed a strand of hair out of her face. "I don't want to see you in danger."

"Well, that's what I want. I told you before: I want you but I don't need you. Erican already said he'd go with me if you don't."

Erican looked puzzled. "I, I didn't ..."

"Shut up, Erican, I know what she's doing." And he did just by seeing the devilish smirk on her lips.

He blew out a breath. "Yes, we can go. I'd love to go to New York with you, Tendra." She beamed at him, making her blue eyes dance.

"But I have one condition," he said. "We need to leave today."

"What? That's not enough time to pack, let alone say goodbye to our friends and your family."

"I'll explain later. Be ready to go in two hours, and you can't tell anyone. Now, go pack what you need and I'll meet you at Launch 42."

She cupped his face, searching his eyes. "What's going on?"

"Please don't ask me why." He gently removed her hands. "Let's just go and be together, forever."

She opened her mouth to argue, but then must have thought better of it. She kissed his cheek. "Okay, baby, let's go." She wrapped her arms around his waist. "I love you."

"I love you too." He wrapped his arms around her, resting his chin on top of her head. "We're going to be okay."

Kellan noticed Callum crossing the room.

Guess he got tired of waiting.

Chapter Six

KELLAN AND TENDRA shifted and stepped their way through the immigration hall along with hundreds of recently arrived Travelers. Kellan felt the pressure of every human gaze in the room. Maybe it was paranoia, but he kept a close eye on the agents.

"Wow, we're here, I can't believe it! Look, there are the pictures of all the immigrants who have come through this island." Tendra pointed to the pictures that filled the walls. Italians, Irish, Polish, throngs of destitute and disheveled who made their way through, who got in.

I.C.E. had set up entry points throughout the United States for the Travelers to pass through and into society. These entry points were heavily protected by agents. If only the world was just as protected for the Travelers. Kellan's people were being attacked in very public places. High traffic street corners, shopping malls, and community parks had become especially dangerous for Travelers. With every new, public attack, it was as if the opposition was sending a vibrant and clear message to Travelers: "Get out." Yet, here he stood, at the door to this world, daring to come in.

If a Traveler had a relation on Earth, then once they passed through the immigration checkpoint, they were allowed to go wherever their relatives were, if they'd have them. But if they were not wanted, then they got placed. Placement was meant to disperse the influx of Travelers evenly into parts of the country so their populations wouldn't be overwhelming. It was really a separation plan meant to keep the potential for violence down, to keep likeminded radicals away from each other for as long as possible. There just weren't enough people who were on the Travelers' side to outweigh the ones who weren't. Police were overwhelmed and couldn't keep up.

There was a third, but risky option. If a Traveler wanted to come to the United States and they had been approved to do so, they could live with a host, a sponsor of sorts who would help them get acclimated to the human way. Kellan and Tendra had a pass to live with the family of an American doctor who Kellan met on the ship during the medical testing. The Marone family had excitedly agreed to host them.

Each step that Kellan inched closer to the front of the line reminded him that those sponsor visas didn't always hold up when the I.C.E. officer had the discretion to reject the pass, another sign of the flawed system where the intolerant could flex influence over the Travelers.

Kellan knew the risks, he was, after all, escaping his father and the life of leadership that awaited him. He was his father's only choice. But there were others who could stand in for Kellan and even though those choices could have negative consequences, it was not Kellan's concern. Tendra was all that mattered to him now. They stood strong with each other, always.

Kellan and Tendra neared the checkpoint, stopping before a metal detector surrounded by heavily armed guards. What did they think could happen? These were just people who wanted to live with them, amongst them.

Ahead of them, a male immigration officer was processing a young female Traveler around the same age as Tendra. She reached for something from her bag and he grabbed her arm violently, twisting it and shoving her to the ground. His bald head was sweating, his face contorted with loathing. He was probably one of the humans who feared the worst and called this an invasion.

Kellan took a step forward to help the girl, but Tendra quickly grabbed his arm. His eyes snapped to hers, which looked up at him with concern. He stayed in line, clenching his jaw. His brashness could have cost them their chance at getting accepted. He took a deep breath, trying to calm his fury. He hoped they wouldn't encounter that specific officer when it was their turn. If anyone touched Tendra, he wouldn't be held responsible for what would happen to them.

Amongst the Travelers, there was a division between those who believed integration was a wonderful gift and those who thought it was only a matter of time before the lynch mobs would start. Some vowed to be prepared to protect themselves when that time came.

The officer did have some reason to be wary of them. There were Travelers who had an ideological view of the new world, ones that saw them as the future, the evolution of species, the ones to eventually take over.

They were the breeders, the purists who wanted to try to protect their genes from the dilution of human DNA. They practiced strict alien-only procreation. They called themselves, "pure" and they were the ones to be worried about. They were the ones with a long-term cause. But they'd never step foot on Earth. Kellan's plan was simple, get in and get to Marone's home, and it was important that Tendra followed it.

"Remember, when they ask us, we say that we don't want to meet or stay with our blood relations and we want to be placed instead here in New York, together. As long as we have a specific residence to go to, they can't deny us, and once we're through, we'll disappear."

"Disappear? Why, when we have a family to receive us?"

"It's complicated, Ten. If we meet that family then my father will always have his eyes on me. Dr. Marone and him are good friends. It's the only reason he's allowing me to go down. Just follow my directions, okay?"

He saw Tendra look closer at the transfer papers he held.

"Kel. What's that say?"

He tried to tuck them away, but she reached in a grabbed them from him, and read them aloud, "You are hereby granted a TEMPORARY visa to enter the United States of America in New York City for a time period of no longer than ... ONE MONTH!"

"Tendra, quiet!" he whispered harshly.

"Why does it say one month? Kellan, is this why you said we had to disappear? What is going on, what aren't you telling me?"

He ignored her and looked forward, eyes stiff on the prize, the exit sign. He had to ignore her or risk drawing unwanted attention.

He scowled at her. "This is serious, Tendra, do as I say."

"I don't like this at all, I'm getting a funny feeling, Kel."

"Next," the officer before them barked.

It was the same officer that mistreated the female Traveler from earlier.

They stepped forward and he held out his hand. "Papers."

Kellan handed the man their documents. "We are Kellan and Tendra."

The officer glanced at the documents and eyed Kellan suspiciously. "Do you desire to reunite with your human genetic relation here on Earth, or do you wish to relocate away from your human genetic relation?"

Kellan fought the urge to wipe his sweating brow. The movement could cost him ending up like that female, and he didn't want to give this human anymore ammo. "We do not wish a reunion with our human family, but we have a host and residence here in New York–"

"Do not call them your family!" the officer spat. "You are a biologically engineered experiment derived from stolen DNA, and that does not make you someone's family!"

"I apologize, officer." Kellan bowed his head. "We do not wish to contact our human genetic relation and would like to relocate to New York City where we have a resident host who will–"

"You there." His focus moved to Tendra.

Kellan stiffened. He didn't like the way that this was going at all, and he didn't like this man looking at his girl.

"Is this true for you as well?" the officer continued.

"Yes." Tendra's voice was quiet and small.

The authority took the papers and stamped them.

"Young lady, you will be headed to Cheyanne, Wyoming, which is in need of population growth. And you... *Kellan*, are going to be relocated to a yet to be determined location." He dismissed them, waving for the next in line. "Next!"

"Wait a minute," Kellan disputed. "We have an established contact here in New York and are only here for one month, you can't relocate us. The New Colonist Immigration Act states that—"

The officer glared at him. "You sir, do not get to tell me about the N.C.I.A. You and your girlfriend are under discretionary review, and by rule of law under article 178.42B of the NCI Act you are being relocated, separately, for an indefinite period of time within which you will either be interviewed and allowed to move to your intended destination or you will be returned to your ship at the end of the thirty day wait."

The news was a dagger to the heart. He couldn't believe this. The humans didn't follow their own rules, yet they expected the Travelers to? He couldn't be separated from Tendra. He wouldn't allow this. Why did he ever agree to coming here? If he'd just stayed aboard the ship with Tendra this wouldn't be happening.

A guard grabbed Tendra's arm, and she looked to Kellan in panic. "No ..." Her voice quivered.

"Don't touch her!" Kellan lunged for her, only to be

stopped by another guard's baton across his kneecaps. Four officers surrounded him and pulled him to his feet.

"Ten!" he yelled, trying to push through and tear himself from their hold.

They restrained his arms behind him and wrestled him toward a door leading away from the station.

"Kellan!" Tendra shrieked.

He caught a glimpse of Tendra being taken through another door in the opposite direction.

"Kellan! Kellan!" She became hysterical, crying, screaming.

An officer smashed a baton across her face, knocking her to the ground.

"*Tendra!*" he screamed.

A stun gun was pressed to his neck. "You think we don't know what you planned to do?" the guard closest to him whispered into his ear. "All of you try the same thing, come down on a vacation visa and then disappear into the ranks of the terrorist groups. We know all about you."

The pain of a thousand pins and needles filled his body. He felt himself crumple.

Then everything went black.

Chapter Seven

TENDRA HELD THE BOAT'S railing, gripping it tighter as she looked out across the water for a sign, any sign that Kellan was okay. She could feel the eyes of the people standing behind her, and gripped the railing even tighter. She was afraid to turn around and face anyone, to face anything without her Kellan. A hand landed gently on her shoulder. Tendra spun around on her heels like she did in the training sessions with Kellan. For a brief moment she thought it would be Kellan since no one, in a very long time, had touched her other than him. But it wasn't Kellan. It was another young man. He was small, closer to her height and had a slim frame, but he had eyes like Kellan's. They were blue against his dark skin, and his smile was warm, very warm.

"Are you okay?" he asked with sincere compassion in his voice.

"No, I'm not. Did you just come down as well?" she asked, hoping a familiar closeness would help her.

"No, I'm not a Traveler."

She stepped to the side to put more distance between them. So far, her only interaction with humans was a man who knocked her out with a baton and another who took Kellan away from her.

He noticed her distance with a sheepish grin. "Sorry, I didn't mean to frighten you, I ..."

"You didn't."

"Right. My name is Daniel, Daniel Marone, and I help Travelers with the transfer from Immigration to their respective transfer stations. I was supposed to meet two Travelers today, my family was going to host them. I only had a description of them though. Are you Tendra?"

Tendra scanned his appearance carefully, searching for any hints of some sort of setup. They'd gotten rid of Kellan, was she next?

Daniel fumbled a bit and produced a badge tucked into his shirt pocket and attached to a lanyard around his neck, "TTRV, Traveler Transition and Return Volunteer." Tendra scanned the credential for a moment. She wouldn't know if it was real or not. Kellan would know though, he would know what to do right now. There was his name though, Daniel Marone.

"Yes, I am Tendra."

"Where is Kellan?" He looked around the ship. "Is he downstairs?"

"No. They took him away." She turned to reveal the dried blood on the side of her head.

"Oh no, what happened, are you okay?" He reached out to touch it, but she turned away, and with a raised hand indicated that he was *not* to touch her.

"Do you have your papers? Maybe I can help."

"Yes, but they aren't the ones ..."

His eyes softened with understanding. "Not where you wanted to go, I bet?"

"No, they took him and are sending me to Wyoming. I don't even know where that is."

"Well it's far from here, but let me see what I can do. Can I have the papers?"

Tendra reluctantly handed them over; what other choice did she have? "Okay."

Daniel took them and disappeared into the crowd of Travelers. Did she make the right choice? Could she trust this Daniel? With no other option, she waited, hoping that she hadn't just been scammed. And for the millionth time, she wished Kellan was here. He would have known what to do.

After a few minutes, Daniel did come back. An older woman, probably in her seventies, trailed behind him. Tendra recognized her from the ship, though not by name. There weren't many elderly aboard. The woman smiled at Tendra and placed papers in her hand. Tendra glanced at them to see the words, "Transfer Permit" and "New York City."

"What? Is this for me? Why?"

Daniel nodded to the woman. "She knows some people in Cheyenne and wanted to go there but was forced to come to New York. So, I had your permits switched."

Tendra looked up to Daniel's smile and smiled back. "Thank you, thank you so much!"

The woman leaned in to Tendra and spoke into her ear, "Go with him. Take this boy's hand for now. You tell the men at the transfer post one thing when they talk to you. You tell them, 'you are welcome.' Think, 'I will pass through.' Trust me, girl, do as I say."

Tendra was confused and concerned again. Before she could ask the woman more questions, she was gone, disappearing into the crowd.

"Wait!" Tendra tried to stop her.

"Don't worry, you'll be fine," Daniel tried to reassure her. "What did she whisper to you?"

She turned to Daniel. Could she go with him? Place her life in the hands of a total stranger–and a human stranger at that. "Nothing. She just said to be safe."

"That's it?"

Tendra forced a grin. "And that I really need to see a Broadway show."

"Huh, that's an odd thing. Well, I'm glad you're all sorted now. Feeling better?"

She grimaced. "No. I still don't know what happened to Kellan, and I don't have anywhere to go. He was handling all of that." She touched her head. "And I'm starting to get a really bad headache."

"Yeah." Daniel looked more closely at the wound. "Let me get you some ice, that's going to swell up for sure."

"Thank you, I'm just ... very, you know ..."

"Alone?"

"Yeah."

"Not anymore. I got you, I'll be right back with that ice and then we'll hatch a plan to find Kellan."

He left, and she was glad. She wanted the ice but she also wanted to be alone. She looked out over the water; they were getting closer to the dock and closer to uncertainty. She was scared, and tired, and just wanted to curl up on the floor and sleep.

Daniel returned with an ice pack. It felt so good

against her skull, like it was putting out a fire burning through her hair.

"I had a thought. You can go to the I.C.E. field office and ask about where he went. I know they have agents assigned to helping Travelers. I'll go with you if you'd like. I can take you to my family's home, get you settled, and when you're feeling up to it, we can go."

Tendra wanted to say no, to tell him to go and leave her alone. With her permit, she had her key to New York, but then what? Where could she go in the city? Maybe staying with Daniel wouldn't be such a bad idea. It wasn't what Kellan wanted for them, but maybe once Ringbak knew that she was there he could help her find out where they took Kellan and get him back.

"Okay," she said.

A grin split his face. She'd never seen a person look so unabashedly happy. "I promise you'll be comfortable and safe."

She could only hope what he said was true.

The boat docked, and Tendra shuffled along with the disembarking Travelers. She warily eyed the agents collecting papers. They welcome the Travelers to the United States of America and seemed just as genuine as Daniel and nothing like the men she encountered on Ellis Island. Soon it was Tendra's turn, and she stepped forward. She didn't have Kellan to protect her this time. She wished he was here to hold her like when they first arrived.

Think ... I will pass through. The woman's words echo in her mind.

Another uniformed agent took her papers, looked at her, and his frown deepened. Did something not match up? Did Daniel trick her? There were no pictures on the papers, just a name and a transfer order. Was the code faulty?

She looked up at the man who was much taller than she and she repeated in her mind, *I will pass through.*

The agent blinked and then smiled and said, "Please pass through, welcome to the United States of America."

She'd done it.

She was in.

She was free.

Tendra walked out of the building, onto the streets of Manhattan. She couldn't believe she had finally made it.

Her elation quickly died.

It all felt empty without Kellan. He'd find her here, one day, under the lights of Broadway, but that day was not today. What would she do until then?

She scanned the horizon one last time for Kellan.

A hand, warm and familiar, clutched her shoulder. Daniel was there again.

"Ready?" he asked.

"Yes, I am," she said but she knew that she couldn't possibly be ready for what she didn't even know was to come.

Chapter Eight

TENDRA WALKED THROUGH the door of a modest yet sophisticated brownstone home in Brooklyn, New York. An older African American man took her things through the door while a woman helped her with her coat and took the bags from Daniel.

"Thank you, son," the man said and then winked at her. "He's almost completed his post-graduate degree, you know."

"Dad."

"What are you studying?" Tendra asked politely as she crossed the threshold to her new life. She looked around. This was what a home, a real home, looked like. Pictures on the wall told the story of a lifetime of experiences that they all had together. A vacation on a beach, a picnic in a park, Daniel's graduation. The smell of real food cooking in the kitchen wafted through the home. The floorboards creaked with each and every new step she took. Everything looked lived in and comfortable. The couch, an armchair, blankets piled neatly in the corner next to a fire place. Music was playing but she couldn't quite make it out. She recognized the songs but a moment passed before she realized she was listening to a record, real vinyl for the first time in her life.

Daniel continued, "Biology, well, sort of, it's ... it's complicated, not that you wouldn't understand, I mean, it's advanced. Oh, that sounds so pretentious, I um ..."

Kellan never fumbled. He always seemed so certain and sure. But with Daniel, she found the act... kind of adorable.

"Sounds complicated," she joked, breaking the tension.

"I'm mapping the Traveler hybrid genome in order to understand how DNA might mutate more quickly in space, or differently, and how that DNA is affected once on Earth for an extended period of time."

She tensed. Too many times she'd seen what scientists on the ship did to Travelers. Was Daniel one of them? She forced a grin. "Well, that sounds fascinating."

"Yeah, well I've had some help." He shot a grin at his father.

"I am the chief terra-scientist on the ship," her father explained to her. "Working with the Travelers in order to understand more about our similarities—"

"And differences?" Tendra interrupted.

"Yes, well it's our differences that make us interesting, don't you think?" He raised his brows in question.

"He's also the first human to touch Traveler skin." Daniel gestured toward a picture on the wall of his father, Dr. Lewis Marone, with Ringbak Arr, shaking hands.

"You know Ringbak Arr?" Her eyes narrowed, she pierced Mr. Marone, with her gaze, trying to keep the hope out of her voice and off her face.

"Ah, there's plenty of time to talk about that later." Mr. Marone waved her off. "Come, let's get you settled."

His smile disarmed her. He was a tall man and she felt diminutive against his stature and she showed it with a slouch and by averting eye contact. She was sure she'd made the whole room feel uncomfortable, but they wouldn't let her know it if she did. They were kind.

Tendra lay in her bed, staring up at the ceiling. The realism of the plaster and paint consumed her thoughts, for a while anyway, until she fell asleep.

The next morning, Tendra awoke to a wonderful smell. She put on the robe that was left for her beside the bed and her own slippers before walking down to the kitchen.

Mrs. Marone was humming while cooking. Eggs, bacon, hash browns–it all smelled so good, and Tendra was starving.

"Sit down, honey, take a load off and relax, I'm about to feed you something gooood."

She was a lovely woman, and Tendra appreciated the warmth.

"Sonny, get her some OJ and coffee, will you?"

"Yes, Momma," Daniel replied with a smile thrown in Tendra's direction.

This was a kitchen, she thought. A small, cozy, used kitchen, and she loved it. From the old and probably outdated wallpaper to the farmhouse sink and the dripping faucet over it.

"Where is Mr. Marone today?" she asked out of politeness. "I'd like to say thank you to him–to you all."

Daniel pointed to the sky. "He's already back up on the ship, your ship."

"He goes up a lot?"

"He's there more than he's here," he whispered to her.

"I heard that, sonny. You better not be disrespecting your daddy. He's up there so that you can be here about to enjoy some of my cooking."

She turned toward them with a tray of bacon, eggs, and hash browns, and it smelled amazing. Tendra thought of nothing at that point, nothing except eating that amazing food.

She would start looking for Kellan soon, she thought, but it was nice to be welcomed in this home while she did it.

Chapter Nine

USING HIS DIRT-STAINED fingers, Kellan forced open his crusted-shut eyelids only to immediately shut them as soon as the brightness of the sun forced its way in. His hands searched the area around him, looking for anything familiar. His fingers brushed along cold, hard asphalt until they hit a bottle, unopened water maybe. He grabbed it and twisted the sealed cap and smelled nothing before taking a sip. It was water, and after taking a large swig, he poured it on his face, washing away the crust from his eyes and the dirt from his face. Opening his eyes again, he looked down at the brownish-red water dripping from his chin into his hands. His eyes adjusted slowly. Brick walls surrounded him, in the distance he could hear low rumblings of motors and people talking. He appeared to be in some dingy, sun speckled alleyway.

"Where the hell am I?" he wondered aloud while attempting to stand, a task much more difficult than it ought to be. "How did I get here?"

Searching his memory made his head hurt. He put his head in his hands as his cheek and head throbbed. He stumbled forward, falling over trash and losing the ragged blanket that covered his shoulders. Finding the remnants of a once intact window, he had a look at his reflection. He was pale, frail, and covered in tiny pin pricks across his forehead, each with their own equally sized bloody scab.

"What the hell?"

The sign on the building at the end of the alley caught his attention: "ANCHORAGE URGENT CARE. EXIT ONLY." *Alaska?*

Why am I here?

He had always wanted to go to Alaska, but not like this. *At least there's a doctor,* he reconciled, making his way toward the rear door, only to stop a split second before his hand touched it.

Scuffling drew his attention to the end of the alley and the men on either side. Across the street, a teenager caught his eye before asking a passerby to take a brief survey. In the street, a cop directed traffic at the intersection. In -between waves, he shot furtive glances Kellan's way. They could just be curious about the man in the tattered clothes emerging from the alley.

Kellan stepped back as a man came down the sidewalk walking a shit-zu. He looked away as soon as Kellan matched his glare. Maybe it wasn't the tattered clothes they had a problem with.

Kellan pressed on, through the rear doors of the urgent care and into a hallway. Emergency exit door alarms blared around him, sending a sharp pain through his head. He winced. *Shoot!* He hobbled down the hall, hitting the walls and passing by the staff. As nurses hollered for him to stop, he bolted down the hallway and straight through the front entrance door, flinging it open and pushing out into the sunlight while people scattered.

Tucked behind a parked van, Kellan could see them all scramble in confusion. The traffic cop, the man with the dog, and the yoga pants lady conferred on the corner, raising hands and pointing fingers, indicating what Kellan suspected. He was being watched. Except for the teenager taking surveys. Maybe he was wrong about that one. *Where did he go? I don't see him*, he thought

The tall teenager with his wavy, brown hair and button down shirt tucked into his khakis was standing before Kellan now. His boots didn't match, they were black, but what made his eyes go wide was the realization that they were military boots.

"You don't look so good, man. Maybe you should see a doctor," the teenager offered, his brows knit together in false concern.

"I'll pass, thanks," Kellan defied. "Who are you? What do you want with me? Did you put these marks on me?"

He raised a brow. "I really think you should get checked out, pal, it looks like you might have lost some blood. Come on, how about you just turn around and head back inside so a doctor can check you out?"

Kellan felt that way too—weak, thirsty, tired.

Kellan looked over the man's shoulder, down the street where the cop, woman, and man who previously had a dog were walking toward them.

"Listen," the teen drew his attention back to him. "Just go to the doctor, trust me."

Kellan lunged at the teen, spun around, and swept the legs out from under the imposter, knocking him on his back.

The man reached behind him and pulled out a taser gun tucked into his waistband. Kellan darted forward, knocking it out of his assailant's hand. With a flicker of metal, the man's other hand punched out a stun gun. It crackled and popped, just like the one in New York. The man drew back, going with it toward Kellan. Kellan twisted his own body around, ducking under the device. He leapt up, wrapping his legs around the man, and pulled him to the ground, knocking him out as they both fell. The approaching attackers paused for a moment before charging toward Kellan.

He ran, fast, inexplicably fast considering how he'd been feeling just a moment ago. He made a series of sharp turns, ducking in and out of streets and alleys, and eventually finding a locked door to an unopened bar called, "The Palace Saloon." He shouldered into the door, breaking it open. He closed it behind him, hiding.

Footsteps drew nearer and then started to fade. He breathed a sigh of relief that none of them seemed to notice the busted door.

Kellan was thirsty, so thirsty. He limped away from the door, making his way behind the bar where he pulled a soda gun from its holster, pressing the button until water streamed out for him to drink. He gulped it down greedily. Thirst quenched, he slumped down behind the bar, utterly exhausted.

He searched the shelves under the bar for anything that could help him, like a bat, a knife, or even a bottle to break, but all he found was a newspaper with a picture of his father on the front page. The headline read, "RINGBAK ARR AND THE TRAVELER EMIGRATI TO SPEAK IN PUBLIC AGAIN." The headline was confusing. Kellan's eyes widened at the date on the paper. It was dated six months from the day he first arrived in New York with Tendra. His breath caught in his throat. How could that be? He was just taken from Tendra yesterday, how could six months have passed? He didn't remember anything past that day.

Tendra, oh my god, what happened to her, where is she?

His heart pounded against his chest.

He curled into a fetal pose on the dirty, back bar floor.

Chapter Ten

"DO YOU WANT me to come in with you?" Daniel glanced at Tendra while he shifted the strap from the backpack on his shoulder.

A small smile curled Tendra's lips. "You're sweet, Daniel, but no."

"Are you sure? How about I come up just in case?"

"In case of what?"

It had taken her six months to get an appointment; she didn't want to do anything wrong and jeopardize it getting pulled.

"I don't know, you know, just in case?" He was sweet, always, and that gave her comfort and moments of happiness. She placed her hand on his cheek.

"Thank you, Daniel, but they said the appointment is just for me, and I don't want to break any rules."

She had so many questions without answers. She wanted to just give up on humans, write them off as monsters that would separate her from her love. But there was something in Daniel's warmth and compassion that still gave her hope for mankind.

Daniel placed his hand over hers on his cheek. She knew Daniel was interested in her, even curious.

More than once she'd caught him glancing her way. So endearing, so honest. Though she'd never admit it out loud, she was not totally unattracted to him; he made her feel good, special, cared about. It felt nice. She couldn't deny it caused her to consider her feelings for him, but she wouldn't act on those feelings, not now, not ever while Kellan was still out there, somewhere.

She loved Kellan and that would never stop. Her memories and hopes for them both kept the spark between them alive.

"Good luck in there," Daniel said. "Are you sure you don't want me to come in with you?" he asked one last time.

"Yes, I have to do this on my own." She grinned at him. "Thank you for bringing me."

"My pleasure." He returned her smile. "Just remember, no matter what they tell you in there, everything's going to be okay, Tendra. We'll find Kellan."

She nodded, but knew deep down that words would only betray her. She raced up the steps to thick, metal double doors. They parted as she neared. She stepped through, and they slid closed behind her with an echoing clang that sent a sense of foreboding down her spine. She took a steadying breath and moved forward down the hall.

She made her way to the waiting area, and her name was called almost immediately, giving her no time to assess the room or the others waiting. Were they Travelers as well? Could they also be looking for lost family and friends?

"Are there many other Travelers looking for missing loved ones?" she asked the woman leading her through the cubicles toward the representatives. The woman stopped suddenly, making Tendra feel as though she'd said something wrong. She leaned in close to Tendra and whispered, "All of them. Dozens every day, all looking for other Travs separated at immigration. It's a real shame." She turned back around and continued leading Tendra down the hall.

Tendra looked back though and saw the hurt and pain in so many eyes, she felt it, empathetic to their shared pain. *It's not right, none of this is right.*

The woman stopped beside a cubicle and waved Tendra in. "Please sit here. Agent Pierce will be right with you."

Tendra took her seat alongside a cubicle desk. All the desks around this one were cluttered and busy, but this one was nearly empty. White, stark white. It reminded her of the ship.

A tall woman with a determined face walked into the cubicle and sat down behind the desk, looking into a brown folder adorned with paper clipped documents. Tendra could only wonder at what the documents contained.

"Hello, I'm Agent Pierce."

"Thank you for seeing me Miss ... Pierce?" Tendra inquired, not knowing the proper protocol.

"Agent Pierce," Kate amended with a tiny smile. "What can I help you with exactly?"

Tendra would have preferred to be dealing with the receptionist, but no luck. Instead she had to tangle with yet another unfriendly human.

"My boyfriend, Kellan, and I were passing through the immigration checkpoint here when we became separated."

"I see that here in your file, but I'm not sure why they've sent you to me," Kate fumbled but recovered, "That is, I'm being reassigned out of this office so I'm not sure why they sent you back to me. I don't think I can help you."

Tendra saddened, her eyes watering.

Kate's eyes softened. "Why don't you tell me what happened, and I'll see if I can get you to the right agent."

Tendra appreciated the agent's effort, maybe this Kate Pierce could be one of the good ones like Daniel. "When Kellan and I came through, we were separated. They took him and put him on another boat. I don't know where he is now, and I am scared, I'm so scared. Can you help me find him, please?"

Agent Pierce picked up the phone. "I'm going to get someone for you right now."

Tendra tried to keep her hope in check.

When no one answered her call, Agent Pierce stood. "Wait here, I'll see what I can find out, give me a minute." Kate moved toward a small office across the room and disappeared behind the door.

Tendra clutched her purse between her hands on her lap. She looked around and noticed that no one was looking up from their desks. She scanned the room for exits, seeing three around the space. A wall of windows on one side of the room could be an exit in a pinch.

At the sound of a door opening, Tendra looked back to where Kate had disappeared to see her returning to the cubicle.

Kate's jaw worked as she reclaimed her seat. "Listen, I don't know what's going on here, but I can't help you, and you need to leave."

Tendra was shocked by the change in her tone. "Why? What did I do? What happened?" she asked, determined not to leave without answers.

Kate waved her off. "I can't get involved in any of this and you probably know that."

"Involved in what? I don't know what you mean."

"You didn't tell me your boyfriend was the son of Ringbak Arr," Kate told her.

Tendra forced her next tear back, and with her shoulders high, she stood just as tall as Agent Pierce. "I haven't seen or spoken to Ringbak Arr since we left. I've tried to contact him many times, nearly every day, but he doesn't respond. Does he have Kellan? Does he know where Kellan is?"

"Of course he does. He's your leader and his son is on Earth. Of course he knows where Kellan is. I don't know what you're planning, but I can't be involved. You have to go."

"Please, I have no one else to turn to. I'm begging you, please help me!" It killed her to beg a human for anything, but she would do whatever she had to do for Kellan.

Kate's brows furrowed. "I can't. Sorry."

Tendra had lost, she felt it. But she still had fight inside of her, she knew that too.

"You people, you humans!" Tendra yelled, causing heads and eyes to swivel in her direction. "You invite us here, you assure us that we'll be safe, welcomed, and free, and then you rip us apart from each other!" She was hysterical now, crying as she screamed at them, "How many others are there like me? How many more are sitting out in that waiting room wondering where their loved ones are, where they went, where they were taken to, and what's happening to them! You are disgusting, you disgust me, you are horrible! Humans are horrible!"

Tendra covered her face, sobbing, unable to keep her tears at bay any longer.

Someone tugged on her arm, and she gasped, looking up at two large, armed men holding her arms. Were they going to take her away like Kellan? She pulled against them feebly as they dragged her out an exit door.

She spotted Daniel waiting by his car parked on the street. He straightened when he saw her. The guards shoved her forward. She stumbled but managed not to fall on her face.

Daniel quickly crossed the street and ran to her side. "Ten! Are you okay? What happened?"

She collapsed onto her knees and sobbed uncontrollably. It wasn't fair to him.

Daniel kneeled beside her and rubbed her back. The comforting gesture only made her cry harder. It should be Kellan comforting her. It should be Kellan facing all this beside her. It wasn't fair.

"We won't give up," Daniel said lowly. But she feared she'd already started to.

Chapter Eleven

KELLAN STEPPED OUT of the passenger side of the idling big rig with nothing but a small backpack slung over his shoulders. He waved off the driver while shutting the door and turned to face the dingy, beat up road leading into Weyknot, Alaska. Hanging in an arch over the entrance to the town main street where the name of the town would normally be were the spray-painted words, "Prospectors go home. No gold here anymore."

Middle of nowhere is where he wanted to be, away from the suspicious eyes that surrounded him in Anchorage.

The town was in shambles, dilapidated, boarded up, and virtually lifeless save for the small watering hole illuminating the early morning air with its neon beer signs. Above the murmur of drunks was the buzz of a chainsaw firing up and screaming to work.

The only other building, if you could call it that, was a small, wooden structure resembling an old office out of a wild west movie. Plain, hand built, uneven board on the landing in front of the door, complete with a hitching post for horses. It had no paint except for the red door frame. The sign above it read, "Trading Post," and as the door opened it revealed a much more high-tech operation going on inside than Kellan would have assumed. Steel cages, gated doors, and display glass made it appear more like a jewelry store in a mall than a trading post on a dirty road in the middle of nowhere.

Kellan continued past the two structures toward the echoing sound of the chainsaw. He rounded a corner to see a man slicing away at a tree trunk with furious persistence, accuracy, and intent. Surrounding him were dozens of carved, wooden statues. There were bears, owls, totem poles, and the like, all in a glorious display of indigenous artistry. These were the works of art that Kellan had read and thought about for years aboard the ship, and they were more glorious than he ever imagined. Tendra would have loved this. He thought about the impossibility of carrying one away on his shoulders—just like he had always envisioned—when he felt something hard pressing against his back. Spinning around quickly, he knocked away a wooden walking stick. He watched it fall and noticed intricate carvings of bears, eagles, and feathers. It have been carved by the chainsaw man from the looks of its quality and detail.

Standing before him were three large, brooding men.

"What choo doin' here Trav'ler?" one of them slurred.

Kellan couldn't figure how he knew he was a Traveler. There were no markings, nothing that would give him away, nothing that this man could see anyway.

"You better get a move on, stranger. There's

nothing for you here." He punctuated his statement with a belch.

Kellan kept an eye on the other two men behind this swaying one. "I'm not looking for trouble. I heard there was a place to rent here, but I don't see a hotel." The men laughed at him.

"There ain't nothing for you here. We said move on," the slurring man insisted.

One of the other men lunged forward. Kellan's reflexes were sluggish from his exhaustion and he couldn't move fast enough to evade the punch. The man's fist smashed into Kellan's jaw, knocking him to the ground, hard. He struggled to get up, his arms shaking with weakness and fatigue.

The men moved closer. Picking his walking stick back up, the belching man raised it above Kellan's head, and for the first time in his life, Kellan was scared. He held his hands above his head, waiting to be struck down.

But nothing happened.

He slowly lowered his arms to find the man staring down at him.

"Run," he was told, with no other explanation.

Kellan scrambled to his feet and raced off into the woods behind the structures and climbed the steep hill that met him. The damp slush of moist ground under his feet sent sharp stabs of pain up his legs. He cried out and fell against the ridge, breathing laboriously. So much pain, still. It had been three days since Anchorage and everything still hurt.

Whatever happened to him back there was making all of his joints ache, but it wasn't like pain from an injury, no, he knew what that felt like thanks to two broken ribs, a shattered femur, and two broken wrists, not to count the endless broken noses. That was the price of training to fight when you were the leader's son. No, these pains were aches, dull then sharp, and transient. Still, even with these pains, he ran as best he could. Why couldn't he muster the adrenaline like he did in Anchorage?

"Why am I so out of steam?" he wondered aloud.

His thoughts were interrupted by a growl, a long deep moan of a growl.

Kellan slowly turned around. Standing on two legs with its paws raised up high was a creature that looked like one of those woodcarvers' statues. The bear was strong and majestic. It was like a dream.

A shotgun blast ripped through the air, dropping Kellan to the ground, chest in the soft dirt. He spun to see a man with a shotgun standing over him. *Did this guy just save my life?* he thought.

"You alright, kid?" the man asked.

Kellan worked himself up to his feet, the final rise assisted by the stranger.

"Thank you," Kellan breathed. "Yes, I think so."

"Good. Name's Buck, but everyone around here calls me Noho. What are you doing up here?"

"I'm Ke ... Kevin, name's Kevin."

"What are you doing up here, Kevin?" the man pressed again.

He stood still, as still as when he arrived. The butt of the gun rested on his thigh, and his hand was placed upon his heavy apron. Kellan recognized the apron. "Hey, I saw you in town, you carve those wood statues, right?"

"They're called totems."

"They're amazing."

Buck nodded, scanning Kellan's clothes and backpack. "So, what are you doing up here, Kevin?"

Kellan turned away. He didn't want to tell the truth, nor did he want to look the man in the eye while lying to him. "I was just coming up for the view."

"The view?"

"Yeah."

"Okay, Kevin, you ready to get away from the view and come back down off this hill? That mamma isn't going to stay away if you don't." He gestured to a small clearing down the opposite slope where two grizzly cubs wrestled each other playfully.

Kellan realized his mistake. "Oh, that makes sense."

"Anyway, I've got to get back to the shop. Why don't you come with me and take a load off? You look like you've been worked over."

The stranger scanned Kellan, and there was no hiding the way he looked. Tattered clothes, dried blood stains on his shirt and pants, bruised face and hands.

"I've got some old clothes you could have, and food's on if you're hungry."

He was hungry, starving, and just wanted to eat. "Yeah, that'd be great, thanks."

"Fine. And don't worry about those drunk idiots, they hassle all the Travs—sorry I know your kind don't like that—Travelers that pass through. They can't punch their way out of a paper bag."

Kellan tensed. How did this man know he was a Traveler?

"Yes ... I've been on hold for almost two hours ...yes, I ... yes, but ..." Tendra sat on the floor of the Marone family living room, next to a warm, crackling fireplace with her stack of papers and folders in her lap, thumbing through them with one hand and holding the phone with the other.

"Yes, I have that right here." She sifted through her paperwork.

"It says specifically to call back today, I even made an additional note of it."

Her frustration and sadness seeped into every word.

"No, no, that's not what I was told ... by ..." She rifled through more notes, forms, and correspondence. "Yes, Mrs. McMillan. That's who I spoke with before. No ... no! I don't need to be transferred, please! Just tell the Ambassador that it's Tendra, Tendra Shadestone!" So strange to hear her say her own last name. Whenever she spoke it, she was reminded that she was not Mrs. Kellan Arr. She should have been by now. If she was, then she would have an easier time reaching her father-in-law, Ringbak Arr, the now, "Ambassador Arr" to the United Nations. She tried so many times, like this time, before to reach him to see if he knew where Kellan was, but she never got through.

"Thank you, I understand, but if you could please just let the Ambassador know that I called again. I just want him to know his son is missing." She always ended it that way but never once did she get a response or a call back. The more times she called, and the more times she didn't get an answer, the more she suspected that they already knew what she was going to say.

Tendra shifted onto her side. She let the papers slide off of her and lay on her back staring up at the ceiling. She was tired. How much longer could she do this? How many more calls could she make? She glanced over at the stack of papers next to her, allowing the weight of her effort to press upon her mind. She must have made two hundred calls and written over a hundred letters in the time since she arrived, alone, cold, and damp.

The fire next to her was warm, so was this house, sometimes. It was a comfortable and safe place but such a sad reminder every day of what she'd lost. She sat next to the fire intentionally. One day she hoped to throw all of those papers straight into the blaze right before she walked out, without telling anyone, and into the darkness, into nothing, into traffic if she could muster the strength. She might have done it already too if not for Daniel. His friendship was the only light in her heart. The rest of the space was filled with anger and sadness. She watched the front door like she always did after these calls, hoping he'd walk in. He always greeted her with a big smile, and it always lifted her spirits, and sometimes it made her feel connected to someone again, even for brief moments, attracted to someone.

Like clockwork, he did come through the door, every day at 7:28 p.m., right after his shift at the Traveler Transfer Station, the same place he helped her navigate almost a year ago.

Daniel didn't disappoint. He smiled when he saw her. He always moved quickly when they were reunited, barely able to retrieve the keys from the antique door handle.

"Hi." He smiled toward her.

"Hi, Daniel." She tried to force one back, but she knew he could tell she wasn't actually happy.

"No luck on the phone again?" he asked as he

put down his messenger bag and moved toward her. "I talked to my father again, but he hasn't seen or communicated with Ambassador Arr in almost two years, ever since he became, well, Ambassador Arr."

"I know. I appreciate it anyway," she replied. Her glance moved from his, staring off into the distance for a moment before looking back to realize she was holding his hands. She quickly pulled them away and felt the betrayal to Kellan. But it felt good to hold Daniel's hands and look at his face, and she hated herself for those feelings.

She needed shelter from the maelstrom of conflict going on inside of her, and as if he could read her mind, Daniel offered one. "I have an idea. There's something I think you'd like to see."

"What is it?" she asked curiously.

"It's a surprise. Get your stuff, will you? Come with me?"

Tendra allowed herself to be released from the conflict for a moment.

"Okay."

"Great! Let's go."

And they did, out the door and into the streets. Tendra looked down again to see that Daniel was leading her by her hand. She didn't let go this time.

She must have been looking down at his hand for a while because it didn't feel like that long at all before he told her to "look up," and when she did she saw the one place she had always wanted to go but never actually took the time to: Broadway.

"Oh, Daniel, it's beautiful." She saw the marquee signs, the plays and musical billboards, the lines spewing out from theatres, waiting for admission.

"I know you were supposed to come here with Kellan, and I didn't want to take that away from him, but I wanted to show you something, something just for us."

Tendra knew Daniel's feelings for her were growing stronger, but he always respected her. "Daniel, I know how you feel, but ..."

"Wait, look up, just wait for it." She saw everyone else around them had also stopped. Everyone appeared to be waiting, holding their breath.

"You see, when someone who was very well-liked or influential on the scene passes away, theatre owners do something special to remember them by ..." He was looking up now, and she knew what he meant. Suddenly all of the lights began to dim, and then one by one they all went out until the entire street, Broadway, was dark.

"They turn out the lights." She smiled as she finished his sentence. She felt the warmth and trust she had in him grow. She held his hand a little tighter and allowed herself to wrap her arm around his, staring up alongside him into the dark night. Then, he kissed her. It wasn't forceful, but it also wasn't weak. It was good, it felt good, and she returned it before pulling away.

"Daniel, I can't."

"I know. I'm sorry. I just ..."

"No, you didn't do anything wrong. I don't blame you. I just ..."

"Come on, let's grab a dirty water hot dog and head back."

"A what?"

Daniel laughed, softening the moment. She

appreciated the tension lifting. He always seemed to know just how to do that.

"A sabrett hot dog, you know, from a cart on the corner. Only thing is ..." He looked around for one. "I don't see any right here. Let's just go down another block or two and see if we can find one. Come on." He held out his hand and she took it. She wanted to go with him, on his adventure, even if she'd never eat something called a dirty water hot dog.

A few blocks down, they spotted a stand, but as they approached, the vendor dropped his umbrella and folded up the cart. "Sorry," he said in a thick, unrecognized accent, "no more." Then he wheeled his cart away.

"Ah, bummer!" Daniel laughingly shouted. It made her laugh too.

"Whatza bummer? You gotta problem?" a strange voice called from behind them. They both turned and saw three men. One had a bat, the other had a bag over his shoulder, and the lead one, the big one, looked like he definitely didn't need a bat, or anything else for that matter. He was big, had to be 6' 4" and at least two hundred and fifty pounds.

"Don't be scared, little girls," he mocked Daniel.

"We don't want any trouble, just looking for a bite to eat, that's all." Daniel looked scared though, and Tendra could feel him start to shake.

"Ain't gonna be no trouble here, we just checking around on things in our hood, you know." The big one stopped a few feet short of them.

"Okay, we'll just be on our way then." Daniel took a step back.

"Just one thing first," the big one said, and Daniel

stopped. "We gonna need to see your button, you know to make sure you ain't one of them Travs." Tendra had been afraid of this. She could tell as soon as they approached that they were looking for something, looking for trouble. Kellan trained her well enough to understand her surroundings and potential threats.

"We're all good here." Daniel put his hand up in an attempt to stop what they all knew was coming.

"All good here? I guess that means you don't want to show them, and if you ain't want to show them then there's only one reason why."

Daniel didn't have time to respond. He barely opened his mouth to protest before the bat came swinging across his face, but was just a hair short of catching his chin. He gripped Tendra's hand. "Run!"

They took off down the street and didn't look back for two blocks. Daniel threw up his arm and with a stiff whistle he hailed them a cab. They jumped in, and he hurried out his address in between breaths. They were safe but in shock. Well, Daniel was anyway.

"I'm so sorry, Ten, are you okay?"

"I'm fine, Daniel. I just don't understand why there are people like that here. What do they want from us?"

"Don't think into it too much. Those are very ignorant and dumb people. They are not the rest of us, you get that right?"

Maybe she did, maybe she didn't, but she dared not tell him what she really understood, that Kellan would have killed all three of them if he was there.

"This is us, right here," he hollered at the driver. They got out, he paid the cabbie, and they approached the steps to his home when a man stepped out from the shadows.

"Hello, Daniel."

Daniel balked. "Excuse me, who are you? What are you doing in front of my house?" He moved in front of Tendra, putting himself between them, and she thought it sweet for a moment.

"And you are Tendra Shadestone?" the man addressed her.

"Look, buddy, you got the wrong house." Daniel was trying to protect her, but she could tell this man wasn't a threat. He had a long, winter coat cinched tight around his slender waist, both hands in his pockets, clearly not looking for a fight. Also, he looked nearly seventy years old.

"Yes, I am Tendra Shadestone. Who are you, what do you want with me?"

"I don't want anything from you, just the opposite. I want to give you something."

"Oh yeah, what's that?" While the man didn't appear overly threatening, Tendra was still suspicious.

"I know what happened to your boyfriend, Kellan. Seems you've been doing a lot of digging lately."

"You know where he is!" Her heart began to race.

"I knew where he was, shouldn't be hard for you to find him from there."

"He's alive!"

"I didn't say that. Look, I have no idea if he's alive or dead or in a coma or living on a farm with a new wife and child, though I doubt that last part to be true. But I know that he was taken and some things were done to him before he was dropped off."

"Things, what things? Dropped off where?"

"Well, I guess I lied. I do want something from you, but I suspect that given the opportunity you have to find this young man and to learn what happened to him, you'll be happy to oblige." Daniel moved in closer to them; Tendra felt him behind her.

"It's alright, Daniel," she placated him. "Okay, what do you want?"

"Your boyfriend was experimented on, like other Travelers who are brought down with the hopes and dreams of a normal existence. He, like them, was taken and had torturous things done to him."

Her natural response was probably one he expected. "What for?"

"Ah, that's the question, isn't it?"

Daniel interrupted, "What makes you think she can help you?"

He turned toward Daniel now. "Actually, I need you both to help. Daniel, it's your father who is doing the testing, and I need you to steal his files for me."

Disbelief flashed in Daniel's eyes. "Nonsense! My father would never do something like that!"

"Of course, you'll need some convincing," he said as he pulled a folded paper from his coat pocket. "Here is a copy of the transfer papers for Kellan." He handed them over, and Tendra grabbed them, scanned them for Kellan's name, and there it was. It read:

TENDRA SHADESTONE: REDIRECT, CHEYANNE WY HOLDING

KELLAN ARR: REDIRECT, CLASSEFIED: REMIT TO XXXXX

"What's this? It doesn't say anything!" she cried.

"It says everything," he responded. "They knew you were coming even though you tried to keep it a secret. He knew you were coming, and he ordered Kellan taken."

Daniel swiped the paper and scanned it with his eyes. "This doesn't say that my father is involved at all!"

"Your father is the one doing the experiments. I promise you'll find that is very true once you dig into his files. It was Ambassador Arr who had Kellan taken. That will also prove to be true from your father's files, and when it does, you'll see that I'm for real and you should do what I ask."

Seemingly finished, the man walked down the steps and past them both.

"How will we find you when we do?" Tendra wanted to know, but Daniel was not as sure.

"Ten, wait a minute. We don't know anything about ..."

She interrupted, "Daniel, please. I need this."

"I'll find you," the man replied before he disappeared down the dark street.

Tendra listened as Daniel unlocked the door, but she was focused on the paper in her hand and Kellan's name in upper case, bold print, right before her eyes.

Chapter Twelve

KELLAN WAS SURROUNDED by the purest white, like the hallways of his ship, but instead of porcelain-like tile, there was semi-solid, crusted snow. He knelt down, careful not to make too much noise as the crunch of the settling snow would surely scare off any game and ensure a ribbing from Buck when he returned empty handed, again.

The stillness, the quiet, and the cold had grown tiresome. He yearned to leave this place and find Tendra in New York. Buck offered to help track her down without alerting anyone to Kellan's whereabouts. Buck was a good friend to Kellan, not just because he let him stay at his house and fed him, but also because Buck didn't ask any questions, especially as to why Kellan was hiding out. Kellan pulled a folded piece of paper from his inside pocket and opened it, revealing a letter. He chuckled at himself for a moment. He felt like he was a character from an old war movie where the soldier pulled out the goodbye letter from his lady waiting back home. But this wasn't much different from that, and just like in the old war movies, this letter, his letter, was worn out. He wondered if he'd ever really send it. Probably not, it could put her in danger from the people who attacked him in Anchorage, but he liked to read and reread it anyway.

Tendra, I miss you so much. I spend far too much time alone, in the woods watching out over nature. It was supposed to be us up here, and for the last few months I've wondered if it will ever be ... us sitting here together. I hold onto the thought that you're okay. Hopefully you've found the Marone family and they've taken you in, kept you safe.

When I woke up, I had no idea where I was or where I had been. I'll explain all of that when I see you but I'm so very scared to put you in danger and I don't know who's after me. I really hope that they're not after you.

I've been following the anti-Traveler protests taking place in New York. They seem to be getting worse, and I hope you're staying safe. The curfews seem to be keeping things from getting too bad, but if they get much worse, I won't be able to stop myself from coming to you, to make sure you're okay. I hope to find out, or to confirm, where you are soon, if that's possible.

I'm not sure you'll ever even read this, I don't know, it just helps me to write to you, to imagine you would read it. The truth is, I'm scared for myself too. I don't know what happened to me, I can't remember anything no matter how hard I try. I even tried some rituals with my host just to see if I could recall anything, anything at all, but all I got was the impression and sensation of floating in a heavy, liquid, purple goo. That's it, nothing else. Some days when I go out to hunt, I sit for a minute and wonder if there isn't a better use of my gun.

I love you, Ten, and I want to be with you and I will find a way for us to be together and to be safe. I promise.

Love, Kellan.

Kellan put the letter away and pulled up his rifle from the crusted snow. He stared at it, he caressed it, he placed it under his chin. How easy, he thought, to just go. He thought about this a lot while out here, but he was never actually able to pull the trigger. Something always stopped him–his thoughts. He would tell himself that this wasn't him, who he was, what he wanted. He felt an external force begging him to pull it, but he always won out against it. Today he was the victor, but just for today. Tomorrow could be a different story.

Kellan crouched, it was still hard for him at times. He still felt pains in his legs, he was still reminded of Anchorage, the pain he felt there. He had still not gained the weight back, and the black circles under his eyes and yellow-ish hue to his skin revealed deteriorating health. He refused to see a doctor though. He couldn't allow himself to be on anyone's radar, not until he had control of his body, which he knew would come after he regained control of his mind.

Through the misting distance and deep into the woods, a young buck, with its head lowered, fed on the grass. Kellan raised his rifle and tried to keep the heavy barrels steady in his weakened hands and arms. Shuffling his feet for stability sent an audible signal of danger to the buck, and as its head raised, Kellan fired and the bullet struck the buck but didn't take him down, and he ran off. Kellan took chase, he had to, he needed this win. The buck was too fast though, especially for Kellan in this state. Still, he continued his pursuit, rushing through the woods and into branches at every turn. Kellan spotted a pass and a ridge above, he could get leverage and jump atop the fleeing meal. Kellan arranged his position and leapt from the hillside onto the animal, but it didn't slow him down, and Kellan was tossed aside, sent rolling down the hill and into a cold, wet river.

On the ship there wasn't anything that could bring Kellan to tears, but this, his complete and total failure to even be able to feed himself was the last straw. Kellan allowed himself to weep as he crawled deeper into the rushing river. As he moved toward the center of the water, he thought of Tendra and imagined for a moment that she was in a beautiful dress, the one she made with the flowers on it and thin enough that when the breeze met her it hugged her perfect body. He saw her smile up close as his hand reached for hers. She stood under a street sign that read, "BROADWAY." And this was enough for him, this was all he needed before the end. He continued his crawl as the water around him covered more and more, his face bobbing under the waves and his right hand outstretched toward his invisible lover. The hand fell, plunging into the icy river and straight down into the mud below. He pulled but couldn't bring it back up. His hand felt stuck, but not under anything, more like a magnet pulling it down. Finally, his weak body had given up on him. This had to be what it was like to die, he couldn't even move his hand—but something wasn't right. He yanked again but he felt his hand being pulled deeper into the mud as if another hand was dragging him down, the reaper perhaps, or Tendra's love helping him to end it all. No, this tugging was waking him. He felt his eyes open wide, he felt his muscles tighten suddenly, he felt awake. Something was giving him energy, was causing his blood to flow with more urgency. He could feel his heart beating out of his alien chest. He steadied his feet, his knees, and dug his heels into the mud, pulling his hand from its captor. He worked with all his might and when he freed himself from this dirty prison, he was shocked to see his hand was not empty, he was clutching something tight in his palm, something that fed him energy and helped him to his feet.

Opening his palm, as the sun streaked across his hand, the glare was undeniable, the rock was recognizable. Gold, a shiny nugget in his hand. That's what pulled him down? How was that possible? It had grabbed him as much as he grabbed it. This wasn't ordinary though, at least not to Kellan. He felt the gold pulsing through his veins, he felt it in his blood. Kellan looked down into the river, into his own reflection, and watched as his sunken eyes returned to normalcy and his pale skin took on a healthy glow. He felt sudden, sharp, deep pains throughout his body, and he screamed, sending the birds flying from their trees. He stood up, tall now with all signs of fragility gone and instead replaced by the stature of the young man he used to be. He looked at the nugget, held it up against the sky. It wasn't massive but it didn't need to be.

He realized two things immediately; somehow, he knew them both to be entirely true. One, the gold was healing him, and two, he could get more of it. Then a third thought–he felt strong, so strong that this third thought was the most important: he could go find Tendra and get them both out of harm's way. He could find her and bring her back to this very river. Even just hearing her voice, letting her know that he was still out here, alive, thinking about her gave him chills. But he knew how dangerous it could be.

Kellan made his way back to Buck's home, stashing his gold under a rock around back before finding Buck at work on his totems.

"Find what you were looking for today?" he inquired.

"I always do."

"Uh huh. Anyway, I have something for you."

Kellan's jaw dropped. "You didn't?!" Kellan's eyes widened. There was only one thing he'd ever asked of Buck: help to find Tendra. Since he was not a Traveler he could poke around without drawing suspicion.

"Lucky for you, I still have friends in the census."

"And? Don't keep me waiting!"

Buck put his chainsaw down beside him and produced a small slip of paper from the back pocket of his dusty jeans. Kellan rushed over at the sight of it, snatching it from Buck's hands.

"What's this, a phone number?"

"New York City. That's where it's registered to. The home of Dr. Lewis Marone, the first handshake guy."

"She made it after all." This news made him smile, he felt warm all over, his head perked up, his back straightened, he felt a rush throughout his healed body. "It's perfect," he exclaimed.

"What's that?"

"Nothing. Thank you, Buck. I owe you a lot."

"No you don't, kid. Just make it back to her. Get yourself in order, and make a plan." Buck took a hard look at Kellan. "You look better today."

"Yeah, thanks to you, I feel great!" Kellan hated lying to the man who had helped him so much, but he couldn't risk anything right now. Anything could stop him from getting to Tendra, and he would not allow that, not at all. He would soon be out of Buck's house, out of his way. Soon he wouldn't be putting Buck in any more danger. All he needed was to get more gold, build his strength up, and buy his way to New York.

It was after two o'clock in the morning when Daniel knocked on Tendra's door.

"Tendra, it's me, are you awake?" he asked through the thick wood.

Of course she was awake, she was always awake, but he didn't know that. She shuffled the papers under her covers. Amongst the handwritten notes were printouts of Traveler headlines and conspiracy websites. She had documents with information on Dr. Marone and Ringbak Arr. She had Dr. Marone's published articles about the genetics of the Travelers. She had a copy of the book, "How to Negotiate with Aliens" written by the mediator who helped to facilitate the Travelers coming down to Earth. The book had sticky paper markers protruding throughout it. She even had one of Daniel's papers on Traveler genetics. Daniel didn't know that she had any of that stuff, none of it. As far as she knew, he didn't believe the strange man and forgot the meeting had ever happened. The truth was that she was mad at him for it, disappointed even. He couldn't defend them against the anti-Trav thugs on the street, and he wasn't going to help her find Kellan or stop the torture of Travelers. She was just going through the motions at this point, biding her time in this house until she had what she needed to go find Kellan. It was a shame, she thought, how close she was starting to feel to Daniel and how quickly he had ruined it. She couldn't totally blame him though, she had lost hope that Kellan was even alive. She didn't know if he was, in fact, alive but maybe he was–maybe.

Anyway, what could he need at this time?

"Daniel, what are you doing?" She looked at the clock. "It's two a.m."

"I need to show you something," he whispered mysteriously.

"What is it?"

He whispered even lower, "Please, let me in. I know you think I've abandoned you and ..." He whispered even quieter, "the man on the steps."

She didn't want to get out of bed. She didn't want to stop going through the material that she had. She didn't want to let him in, but she did anyway. Hunched over, she slumped to the door and unlocked it, then slid back under the covers.

"Come in."

He did, holding a manilla envelope. She noticed it had something stamped on it, but she couldn't make it out. Now she was curious.

She motioned for him to shut the door.

"I need you to see something." He showed her the envelope, and she could now see the stamp clearly: "CLASSIFIED: TOP SECRET"

"Daniel, what is that?"

"This came tonight, a courier brought it to the house. For my dad."

"Your father hasn't been here in almost a year."

"I know. I hacked his email, his personal account."

Tendra shot up. Why would he have done that unless...?

"I know you think I didn't believe that man and that I didn't want to help you, but I just didn't want you to get in trouble."

She perked up, couldn't believe her ears. She

was wrong about him, wasn't she? "Daniel, what did you do?"

"I've been going through his work, his papers, his files, and I found a few things, but nothing made sense, it was just data. So I hacked into his personal account, thinking maybe there would be something in there even though it's not his secure government account. Who knows?"

"And?"

"It paid off. Last night he got an email that was sent to his personal account by mistake and it was marked urgent, that this packet needed to get to him. So I replied and said to drop it at the house right away."

"Oh, Daniel."

"And then I deleted the email. And tonight, it came."

"You opened it?"

"Immediately."

"Daniel, I ..."

"I didn't want you involved in any of that, you could get in a lot more trouble than me if you were caught. And besides, I wanted to understand all the data I had found."

"And?"

"It's bad, Tendra, real bad."

Tendra stared at the broken seal. Her tone shifted on purpose. "Tell me."

"The Traveler children," Daniel continued, "the government, the United Nations is abducting them, and when they eventually are returned to their families, they are changed, tired and sickly. The ones who do come back anyway ..."

Tendra grabbed the folder that had the intel and scanned through it. She didn't understand the technical info, and there was a lot, but she did recognize one thing–Dr. Lewis Marone's name, everywhere.

"Daniel, I don't understand this. What does it say?"

"The children are initially brought to their attachment families, but then they are abducted and brought back to the ship and they undergo a battery of invasive tests."

"Testing for what?"

"It doesn't say. These figures only indicate positive and negatives but what they are testing is purposely omitted to keep the study blind. But one thing is for sure, my father is involved and knows more than we thought."

"Daniel, is this really possible? He's your father."

"It is, it's all right here, every gruesome detail, it's all here, the mission brief, the protocols, and worst of all, the place where my father's signature is meant to approve the measures they're using."

Tendra sunk to the floor, back pressed against her bed frame. She sobbed, thinking of the children she'd cared for over the years, the ones she loved and who loved her back, and the thought of them being tortured was painful, it in itself was torture.

"Why would they do this, Daniel?"

He shook his head. "I don't know, but it's not all bad news." He rifled through the pages and held the document up to her.

"What is that?"

He ran his fingers down a column of numbers.

"These numbers are identification markers of the children."

"Why is that good news? I don't understand."

Daniel paced the room excitedly. "Think about it,

we can stop them by preventing them from reaching these kids at all!"

"So we're supposed to find their parents and tell them? Then what? They'll be powerless against your government."

"No, you don't understand. These are the children that are still here, on Earth, these are the ones that they plan on taking, and these dates are when they are going to do it. We just need to find a way to get to them first!"

She felt a burst of promise fill her heart. "So if we can get this information out, then they can be stopped before it's too late?"

"Yes! Exactly! We just need to get this to the right people or Travelers who can make it happen."

Tendra sank back down to her pillows. She knew what he meant now.

"You mean the terrorists, don't you? Daniel, I don't know, they're killers."

"Who else then if not them? Who will save your children?"

She knew he was right. They didn't have another choice. Their only option was to funnel the info to one of the Traveler terrorist groups who hated the humans and wanted their own freedom. If they had this, maybe they could save the children before it was too late.

Chapter Thirteen

HIGH UP IN the hills above town, he walked the running streams and creeks that had been mined for a century by gold-hungry scavengers looking for their big payday. A big payday never came for anyone in this town, and everyone laughed at Kellan when he bought his first gold pan before setting off, fully unprepared. When he returned three days later with a few hefty nuggets, the laughter quickly turned to resentment. Being a Traveler only made things worse. The townsfolk, mostly Inuit, were sure that he was using some secret alien technology or powers to find the gold. They thought it unfair. They hated it so much that some of the men followed him into the woods on more than one occasion, jumping him on his way back down, stealing his gold. Not today though, not ever again. That ended fast, and after sending his stalkers back down bleeding and limping, they stopped taking his gold.

Kellan watched his feet and carefully made his way down a frozen sheet of ice. Step by step, he thrust his oversized snow boots deep into the crust, cracking each fresh sheet of ice and snow. With every step he was closer to Tendra, he felt it. He felt her. It would be their time again, he was sure of it.

Settling down next to a running stream, he took a moment to breathe in the fresh Alaskan air, real air, not recycled air like on the ship. It was the same, chemically speaking, he knew that, but it tasted different, if that was even the right word for it. Actually it was the lack of taste, now that he thought of it. The air on the ship had a kind of artificially sweet taste. Anyway, enough of that, there was work to be done, and Kellan had to keep his mind on the task at hand. He found comfort in the thought that soon enough, what was happening now, what he was living through now would soon come to pass. He had Tendra's address and her phone number now, and he had a plan to get back to her and to take her away with him, far away.

First though, he would find more gold, and that's what he did. With his gold magnet hands, he effortlessly pulled more and more from the ground.

Kellan looked at today's haul, it wasn't much, a few flakes and a couple of nuggets, but it was all he needed to get him to Tendra. He chuckled. His pan lay untouched in the snow beside him. His hands sat in the water, just above the dirt, gliding effortlessly against the stream. He laughed at how right they were about him. They had no idea. Neither did he, really, and he was aware of that.

He put his hands in the water, moved them around, and like a magnet he watched them drop when gold was underhand. An alien trick indeed. Maybe a gift from their creators. He wondered what other gifts his kind had. Were there farmers growing crops in infertile lands, fisherman pulling in great hauls from the barren seas, stock brokers pulling off impossible trades?

His hands fumbled in the mud, and he pulled them out like a dual handed scoop. A nice, little nugget shined atop his palm. He thought, *A few hundred bucks at least.* Well, anywhere else a lot more, but they hated him here and they showed it by paying way less than they should for his gold. But at least he didn't have to hide it anymore.

No one liked the Travelers, Kellan was sure of it. His only experiences with humanity thus far had been tortuous. Losing Tendra was one thing; he knew he would find her. The guard who separated them didn't know or care about either of them. Kellan would never forgive that guard for ruining his life, for taking Tendra away, for sending him to this hellhole. Someone hated him enough to take his memories and then dump him in Anchorage. Everyone here hated him, and they never let him forget it. To these Inuit, he was another white man come to take from them, and they didn't want to wait to find out what he would take. Everyone hated him, except Buck. Kellan admired Buck and even started to imitate his look, his beard, his clothing, and his tough exterior.

Kellan had become husky and bearded, with the pelts of his kills adorning his body, and he liked how the strength made him feel. Like he could tackle whatever tried next to keep him from Tendra. He pushed his rifle behind him, and his satchel bounced against his leg as he walked. He pulled a canteen from it and swallowed down a few gulps of water before stopping at the sound of movement. Kellan wasn't a real tracker yet, but he didn't need to be to spot the three Inuit approaching.

Jomo was the fat one who lead the group. Kellan never started anything with Jomo, but Jomo liked to get in Kellan's face at the trader's shop in town. Blunto was also fat. To Kellan, they were all fat, slow, and lazy, that's why they always came in threes when they hassled him. Jomo and Blunto were gross men with shiny, perfect ponytails. Something that always made Kellan laugh when he saw them. That laugh was probably why the fights always started so fast.

The third man was new, Kellan didn't recognize him, but he was big, bigger than the other two and probably much faster too.

Why follow him here, the top of Mother's peak, a cliffside a few miles outside of town? All their run-ins so far had been in town. From up here, Kellan could hear the chainsaw whirl coming from down below where Buck was putting on his daily show. What would Buck do in this situation, he wondered. Kellan glanced over his shoulder, down the cliffside. It was far too steep for him to climb down. The only way was around these three goons.

Kellan was ready for all of them, anytime. Still, this new guy was big and mean-looking, enough to make Kellan wonder if he was a real threat or not. Kellan caught a tattoo under his eye and one around his neck that depicted a pair of hands made to look like they were strangling him. Who does that to themselves?

"Flesh bag, what you doing up here alone again? Don't you know there're things that'll kill ya?" Junto leered at him.

"Yeah, and if the wolves don't get you, maybe an avalanche does or at least a bad spill down the hill here and into them rocks there. Then who knows what happens to that gold," Blunto so eloquently added.

"You might even get pounded and be left up here to die," the choker warned.

The guy with the choker tattoo was the first to move. He lunged at Kellan, raw power and no elegance. Kellan was able to sidestep and shift enough to avoid a direct blow, but then the fat ones came from both sides; they too were easy to sidestep.

Something hard and heavy collided with the side of Kellan's head, rattling him and blurring his vision in a blast of pain. The snow cushioned his fall, and he shook his head, blinking to try to regain focus.

Kellan swiftly rolled over to avoid another hit and reached over his shoulder for his rifle.

Junto's victorious smile was replaced by a look of heavy fear. What little blood remained in his face drained at the sight of the monstrous Grizzly bear standing ten feet tall, claws out, above them all.

The three men were frozen, but Kellan felt a surge of energy that propelled him to his feet. He jumped back fast enough to grab his rifle and land just out of the reach of the monster's swipe. He smiled. He liked this, and the others saw that. They saw Kellan's smile and it paralyzed them even more, which was good because Kellan needed all of his focus on surviving this bear. Kellan stared down the living mountain. He knelt down on one knee, placed both hands on the ground, and stared, really stared, up at the bear.

The ground must have started shaking by the looks of the three men losing their footing and falling down. Kellan had caused that, but he didn't understand how. Next, the air grew warm, the taste of real air faded, and a burning scent took over. The bear made a move on the three defenseless, grounded men, but before he could hook his massive claws in them, Kellan jumped up. He leapt into the air and cocked the rifle as he flew toward the side of the grizzly. In a swift motion, he raised the rifle, and when he reached the same height as the bear's head, he fired, releasing a single shot into the left temple of the animal. It caused instant death. The blood floated out into the air and fell with the body, landing on top of the frightened men. Kellan lifted the bear's head off of them.

"This guy belongs to me. We can all agree on that, yes?" he stated. It was not a question.

The men responded, in unison, anyway, "Yes."

Chapter Fourteen

KELLAN EXITED THE trading shop and stuffed some money into his pocket.

He was done.

Kellan laughed.

Tendra was in New York City, and it was time to go get her. *Broadway.* That was where he would meet her. That was where she always wanted to go.

Kellan stepped out onto the muddy road and walked across the street to where Buck was carving out his latest statue. Kellan watched as sawdust spread across the sky like golden snow. It truly was mesmerizing to watch Buck swing his metal brush, even if he had no hope of ever selling one of his masterpieces in this town. The people here could never afford one. Even if he wanted to trade, they had nothing.

Across the road, townsfolk stopped what they were doing to watch Kellan like he was some kind of freak. He could feel their stares but didn't care, it was time to move on.

Buck caught a glimpse of Kellan and turned off his chainsaw. "This is it then?"

Kellan nodded, but shot him a quizzical look. "How'd you know?"

"Your smile, kid. It gives you away. This is the happiest you've looked since you first rolled into town. You ready for what you're getting into?"

"Ready or not, it's time. Can you do me a favor first?" He reached into his pocket and pulled out a handful of the bear's claws. "Can you do your thing with these?" Kellan pulled out a wad of cash from his other pocket.

"Kellan, I'm not going to take your money for this, you know that, right?" Buck responded, taking the bear claws as they spoke.

"Buck, you've put me up, shared your food with me, and taught me how to survive out here, all the while not asking for anything from me. And might I add I haven't seen you make one dollar since I've been here."

"Still, I don't want you to–"

"Please, let me do this," Kellan insisted.

Buck gave him a reluctant nod and took the money.

Chapter Fifteen

"THE CROWD IS getting bigger." Tendra wrapped her arms around Daniel's waist as they both peered out the window of his house. Small groups of three or four at a time hurried past the house, moving toward something, something that was gathering at the other end of the block. Within seconds they all converged in front of Daniel's house.

One of the passersby shouted, "In there! Doctor of our demise, come on out!" They were after Dr. Marone because he worked closely with Ambassador Arr to help bring the Travelers down to Earth. Some, like the men outside, hated him for it, and they wanted him to answer to them, they wanted him to come out but, as usual, he wasn't there. Tendra was, and if they caught her, they'd kill her, she knew it.

"We're safe in here, it's like a fortress, my dad made sure of that when he first started traveling up to the ship. No one can get in."

Daniel looked deep into her eyes; she could feel him penetrating her soul. Tendra could hardly believe how close she'd become to him and how much she'd come to rely on him. Her arms around him was something she couldn't have imagined last year, but now seemed as natural as breathing Earth air.

"Let's go, you two," Daniel's mother interrupted. "Down to the cellar, let's get you into the safe room."

Tendra had no intention of going down there. Once she did, it would be hours, probably the next morning before she got out.

"Okay," she responded, "let me get a few things."

"There's no time, haven't you two been watching the news?"

Of course she had be watching the news. In the last few months, the anti-Traveler sentiment had been growing, but since the explosions during Ringbak's speech there hadn't been any other large-scale attacks. Still, Travelers were being cornered in the streets by angry mobs insisting people reveal their mid-drifts to show if they had three belly buttons or one–just like they had done to her and Daniel. Show that you have three or don't show at all and expect to get knocked down and have your clothes ripped off while your body is checked and then beaten, sometimes to death.

Daniel flipped on the news in the kitchen while they packed up some food to take down to the shelter.

The banner along the bottom was simple and clear: "Attacks on Travelers up 200% in the last four days. Hundreds expected to be harmed this week."

"This is bad, really bad," Tendra remarked, eyes frozen on the screen. Daniel hustled to get food into bags while Mrs. Marone hurried around the house grabbing valuables and sentimental belongings.

"The police will be here soon, but we need to get downstairs until they arrive!"

She'd never seen Mrs. Marone this serious around her. She was scared.

Three crackling bangs popped through the air, dropping them all to the ground. The windows on the front door displayed three bullet strikes.

"It's bulletproof, they won't get in with that, but they could have something stronger coming." Mrs. Marone lifted herself up and grabbed Tendra by the hand, turning her eyes and attention away from the door.

"Let's go, honey. Daniel, let's get going."

Tendra pulled herself up when she felt the buzz of her phone in her pocket. She pulled it out, stopping herself and Mrs. Marone for a vulnerable moment and saw the text from an "Unknown Number" that simply read, "BROADWAY." Her heart racing, she tucked it away and walked away with Mrs. Marone but forced herself a look out the window where she could see a growing crowd, people yelling, and one sign that she could make out through the frosted glass. "Traitor" was all it said. Now she had to hide downstairs, but the fear of doing so outweighed her fear of the crowd.

She looked back down at the phone. This could be it, the meeting with the mysterious man who knew how to find Kellan. They'd been waiting for him to contact them, for the trade, information on the experiments in exchange for information on Kellan. And now she had it, real documents, real proof of the program.

"What is it?"

"Daniel, I ..."

"Is it him?"

"I don't know, it might be, it could be. I have to go, I have to bring him the proof."

"If you give that to him then we can't save those kids, you get that don't you?"

"We don't know that; he might be able to help–"

"Don't be naive, they're all the same, and the second he has that document he's going to trade it in for something for himself. It's just blackmail, I'm sure of it."

She didn't care. She had already decided that she'd give him what he wanted. She owed it to Kellan, and as much as it pained her, killed her, to think of the children like the ones she cared for on the ship being hurt, she had to do this for Kellan. He would do it for her, and knowing that fact kept him alive to her.

"You could be killed if you go out in that mob right now," Daniel persisted.

"Daniel, please," she begged, holding his hand tight, her eyes piercing his furrowed brow. "I need to know what happened."

"And what if it is him and he gives you what you want? What happens to us? Will you just leave me, after everything?" He was hurt, and she knew that too. She wished she could just walk out into the mob and let them do what they wanted to her, anything to stop the hurting, her and Daniel.

Tendra realized the gravity of the moment for them both. She could see by his downplayed chin that while this may have been the day she'd been waiting for, this was the day he'd dreaded.

As the crowd grew larger and louder, Tendra felt the conflict inside as deeply as she felt the noise from the outside.

"I will be back, I will come back, and we will figure it out, I promise." Her voice softened just enough to still be heard. She took his hand and held it in her own, to his cheek. "I am going to let him know about us. I will explain how much has changed since immigration. It will be fine, I promise."

"No. Don't make me that promise. If you come back, it needs to be because you made that choice when you find out if he's alive, not now when it's just you and I here."

Daniel helped Tendra with her coat and opened the back door for her. Still a gentleman right up until this moment, the moment that he might lose her forever.

She felt him grab her wrist, spin her around, and then he kissed her. She kissed him back, deeply, longingly, with pleasure and with contentment. She let out a slight moan and sigh then pulled back and touched his face.

"Ten, I ..."

"Don't. Wait until I'm back." She left, pulling her hood over her head as she slipped out the back door into the darkness.

Chapter Sixteen

TENDRA STOOD UNDER a lamppost eagerly anticipating meeting the strange man. She knew what she told Daniel, but now that she was about to find out what happened to Kellan, all of her feelings for him had returned.

As she walked, the breeze hit her just enough to flutter about her body, allowing her dress to hug against her buttocks and her crotch. She wondered if everything about her was just how Kellan remembered, just how he left her.

Men didn't just look, they stared. Tendra knew, though, that she wasn't that same girl. What about Daniel?

The conflict was painful, the feelings too hard to reconcile. She had to be prepared if that time came, but she saw that wasn't going to be possible, she had just run out of time. Kellan surprised her, coming from behind and kissing her on her neck below her ear, making her shiver. She knew it was him, and was instantly flummoxed, weak-kneed. This was no dream, here he was, and he was holding her just the way she had hoped. She turned around in his arms.

"Kellan?!"

He was always a big guy, but now he looked more, well, jacked. His shoulders were so broad and muscular, his back was so straight, and his face looked as chiseled as ever except for the slight wind burn effects on his nose and cheeks.

They locked eyes, and she dissolved into tears. He pulled her to him, and they held each other tight for what seemed like hours.

"It's so amazing to be back in your arms, to feel your hands once again. You're all I've thought about," he said.

"I can't believe you're really here! I wasn't expecting, I didn't think—"

"You look the same as when I left you, except for this curious tattoo. When did you get this?" He brushed his fingers over the marking on Tendra's neck. This was the tattoo marking of the Travelers who did not want to blend in and be mistaken for everybody else. It was their symbol of alien blood or extraterrestrial origin. It was a triangle with three distinct points. It revealed their identity, proudly.

His brows pinched. "You know that there are people who don't like us. If they see this, they'll kill you!"

"I know. It wasn't like this when I got it; it was just a symbol of pride."

"Things are bad. I saw it, Ten, all across the country, all across the world. They hate us." She could feel his sadness, his disappointment in everything that was supposed to be. He cried. He never cried, but still, he cried.

"Kellan, a lot has changed." She touched his cheek.

"Where were you all this time? I've missed you so much."

He brushed back his tears, perked up, and held out a gift for her, a gold necklace which he promptly placed around her neck. She obliged. "Oh, Kellan, it's beautiful. How did you afford this?"

"I didn't buy it, my love. I've spent the last year digging for gold, and I made this for you," he professed proudly.

"Kellan, I ..." She wanted to tell him to stop, to wait, to take a minute, a moment to breathe, to think, for her to tell him what had been going on, for her to tell him about Daniel, like she promised.

"That's not all I have for you." At those words, she stopped him before he could pull anything else from his pocket. He had to know the truth.

"Kellan, stop," she insisted softly.

"What is it?" He searched her gaze.

She pulled him into an alleyway, away from the sounds of shouting and gathering. The angry mobs were forming in the distance around them. "Kellan, there is so much I need to tell you, and you may not like all of it, but I'm yours, I'm here and I'm all yours if you'll still have me."

"Still have you? Ten, you're all I've thought about, what are you talking about?"

The sound of metal being dragged along asphalt reverberated from behind them.

They both turned quickly to see a group of men approaching from the end of the alley, lugging aluminum baseball bats along the ground and alley walls as they approached.

One of them called out, "Show it to us and we'll pass right by."

"They want to see our stomachs, to see if we're human. Tendra, don't move."

They approached, and Kellan moved away from Tendra toward the men.

"Kellan, don't—"

"It's okay, I've got this. Just stay back." He was acting like a man, a protector for her, but she knew what he didn't, that these guys were the same ones that she and Daniel had encountered, and they already knew she was a Traveler.

"Be on your way and there won't be any trouble," Kellan declared, making a show of his strength.

The men surrounded Kellan and Tendra. They stared at her.

"I guess that's a no then," Kellan deadpanned.

"Hey guys, we know this one, she was here with her boyfriend, making out in the alley, remember?"

And there it was. Kellan turned to her, she could see it on his face, she could see the betrayal.

"Ten, you know these guys? What are they talking about?"

She didn't get to answer, though she tried. "Kel, I—" But he had already turned back toward them.

Kellan rushed, they all rushed, and Kellan swung and hit the first man clear across the jaw. Another grabbed Tendra and held her while a third punched her in the stomach.

"NO!" Kellan screamed, reaching out for her.

One of the men used the moment to his advantage and struck Kellan across the face with a baseball bat.

Another bat smacked across Tendra's face, knocking her to the ground. A sharp, dizzying pain and partial blindness disoriented her vision. She fought to concentrate, and her vision slowly cleared to reveal Kellan on the ground being kicked, punched, and beaten with the bats.

After a moment, the men left him to bleed on the ground. They sauntered toward Tendra, grabbing at her, pulling her up off the ground, and holding her up while she tried desperately to regain control of her limbs and her breath.

They ripped off her purse, then her necklace, using it to choke her for a moment before it snapped and flew to the ground in pieces. She bent and crawled to pick up the bits, but her position was used against her and she was grabbed by three of the men as they ripped the pretty dress from her body, shredding it as they pulled it from her.

"I knew it! She's one of them. Invader!" a man called out as they saw her bare stomach and the triple markings of a Traveler.

Kellan gathered himself and stood. He lunged at them, punched one, kicked another, and then fell to the ground with another man's neck in his arms, snapping it.

Tendra punched one man and roundhouse kicked another. Arms came around her from behind and a sharp knife pressed against her bare stomach, slicing her across her alien belly buttons.

Blood spilled.

Kellan screamed and lurched forward, losing a step. They knocked Kellan down. They held him down as Tendra lay on the ground. He stood again, moving toward her until he was knocked on the back of the head with a bat. He fell right next to her, his jaw crushed along the asphalt.

Tendra crawled to Kellan's side. He reached out to her and she reached back to grab his hand and hold it; she was still alive, but he was lifeless. A puddle of blood was building around his head. She held his hand but felt something: he was holding on to something–four throwing knives. His death drained whatever was left of her innocence. She was nothing but rage now.

She stood, using all the adrenaline she had coursing through her. She checked her stomach, it wasn't bad, just a flesh cut.

She bent back down to Kellan, her tears the only sign of her humanity, that half of her anyway–there was that other part, the alien part too, though, and she felt it now. Over him she wept, her hand on his heart. Each tear that dropped from her cheek like hot oil from a frying pan, dripped onto Kellan's chest, instantly burning small, pinpricks of holes into his shirt. She pulled away at the sight of what she was doing to him. Her hand left his chest, but a handprint remained in his skin, her brand on his body; her perfect, petite hand. She hated those hands now, the ones that Kellan loved so much. She rose as she pulled away, looking up to realize there were more of them, at least five more assailants, and they were watching her. She knew that they wanted to kill her. But she wasn't running this time, and they were woefully unprepared for what was to happen next.

Sorrow and anger grew inside of her. She moved away from Kellan. She surveyed her surroundings.

Men gathered around, they whispered to each other, looked at her, and in a split second, no more than the time it takes for a short breath, they came for her, charging with blind rage.

Tendra stepped back, retreating upon instinct, but her red running shoes brushed up against something metal—it clanked. On the ground lay the knives Kellan had given her.

Tendra bent down into a runner's starting line stance, grabbing the knives, two in each hand. She pounced up from the ground into a spin, arms extended at her sides like a horizontal windmill. She released the daggers, and they landed in the hearts of the attackers on either side of her. She landed on her feet, and all the men around her collapsed to the ground, motionless.

She took one last look at Kellan and then she turned and ran, disappearing into the streets, stopping only long enough to see the crowd gathering around Kellan's body and the handprint that sat atop his chest.

PART 2
AGENT
KATE PIERCE

Chapter One

KATE WAS ALONE.

She lived alone.

She worked alone.

It was how she functioned. It was what made her a good agent. No attachments. No pain.

She shifted her position from atop a doctor's cold, examination table and dropped her bare feet onto the even colder floor. She paused for a moment to look at herself in the mirror on the back of the door. She met her striking blue eyes and took in her runner's physique. She should have smiled back at the person she saw. But she didn't. She interrogated the stranger before her with a silent and disinterested gaze before pulling on her slacks and her comfortable, form fitting blouse. She donned a standard issue baseball cap and windbreaker jacket provided to her by the Immigration and Customs Enforcement, known by its acronym, I.C.E.

She caught herself once more in the mirror and quirked a brow. She looked more like a disaster victim who'd been given the jacket to take comfort in–not an agent. That's what the jacket was to her: comfort, protection.

To comfort her from what, though?

She was supposed to be a hero, a protector, that's why she'd signed up in the first place, that's what she'd trained for, that's what she gave up her twenties for. She just hadn't had her chance to prove it yet.

She opened the door and peered into the hallway looking for the doctor instead she saw a young mother, about her age, pushing a stroller. She and Kate looked alike in many ways. They were both young and fit and they both wore running shoes. The big difference though was that the young mom smiled and Kate did not. Also, Kate didn't have a child. She wanted one but she wasn't even in a relationship let alone pregnant. She closed the door and sat back down.

Three subtle knocks on the closed door indicated that the doctor was back. He entered, staring down at his notes, too rushed to bother with eye contact. Other patients to help.

"There is no news," he told her. "We'll run more blood tests, but I wish I had more to add. We can try some new tests out, see if there's anything we can find this time around that didn't show up before but to be frank, I don't think you'll be able to bear children, even with the new procedures coming out. In the meantime, remember you are young, in excellent shape, and otherwise perfectly healthy. Other than these bouts, of course."

Kate cringed at the word, "bouts." But that's what they were: seething stomach pains followed by a sudden burst of hell behind her eyes. Then tiredness, total bone tiredness. They started out once or twice a year and were now almost bi-monthly occurrences.

She sighed. Still no answers. "I didn't want kids

anyway. Thank you, doctor." She lied. He could tell, she could tell by his sunken brow.

He tucked his clipboard under his arm and offered her a sympathetic look. "The speech today ... I'm sure it will be–well, I can imagine that anyone in the federal government will have added stresses in the coming weeks. Try to rest when you can, keep exercising, and we'll get to the bottom of what's going on, okay? Just give it time."

Time. What a funny word. It'd been four years since the aliens had arrived. Travelers, they called themselves, and today one of them was setting foot, for the first time, on Earth, here in New York, her city.

"Thank you, again, doctor. If you'll excuse me, I have to go. We are expecting some increased activity at our offices today."

"Of course, all hands on deck, right?" He offered a compassionate smile.

Kate made her way out of the examination room and moved hurriedly down the halls and into the street. She passed throngs of people all moving in the same direction, toward a view of the Liberty Island where Ringbak Arr, the alien leader, would be speaking. Kate headed the opposite way, toward her office, the Immigration and Custom Enforcement headquarters.

At her job, she dealt with the ones that no one wanted to help, the people who weren't sick, disabled, or destitute, but just unfortunate, poor, and burdened . . . Now, with the immigration of the Travelers, the human migrants in need had to wait even longer. The long lines of desperate and downtrodden foreigners that Kate encountered waited a lot longer than four years to get into this country, she just didn't know how to help them. She sulked as she stared at the tired faces of the men, women, and children, some teary eyed from the exhausting wait and uncertainty. They wanted little more than to come into the country and be given the basic right to the pursuit of happiness.

Kate took after her father, Severin Pierce. She liked to remember him as a man with a romantic view of equality and peace throughout the world. The one thing that her father wanted was to see those who couldn't take care of themselves be taken care of. Her father would pace the circular rug in the living room of their modest row home and fist the day's news in his hand, espousing frustration with politics. For Kate, that was love. She saw it early on, a man who wanted to help.

Now, Kate sat behind her desk, with her sidearm bearing no signs of use. She was no one she wanted to be, and she was what she'd hoped she'd never become. She stared down the line at the very people her father hoped would someday fall upon the good graces of a society that valued their health and happiness at least enough to give them a fair shake. It was a dream that carried Kate into service and the beginnings of her career as an immigration agent. Except this line of coughing mothers overburdened with children and baggage and men beaten down and surrendered to bureaucracy wasn't what she had envisioned at all.

She was living a life that made her question her father. Maybe he was wrong to want to help.

When you're a kid you believe your parents can do anything, and she believed he would make a difference, and she'd seen the world the way that he wanted it to be: just, kind, fair, peaceful. It was none of those things, and she knew that by the time she was twelve. One night at dinner, sitting around the mid-century table and chairs that she grew up with, the ones that were cool when she was a kid but looked dilapidated, old, and poor as a teenager, she told him he was naive to think the world was a good place and that people were kind and that life was fair.

She'd told him outright, "It can't be all of those things, and no matter how much you want it to be, wanting it isn't enough to make it so."

He'd smiled at her though, as if he'd been waiting for her to eventually make that realization herself and offered simple advice, "You want to be happy in life, kiddo, then all you need to remember is this: Intelligence and happiness can go hand in hand if you understand that holding two opposing thoughts in your head at the same time is possible. 'What it is right now is not how it will always be,' for example, helps us to see past the temporary situations of sadness, pain, and injustice because we know that these things can, and will change."

"I don't think that's what that means, Dad." It probably didn't, but his optimism was disarming, even to a pre-pubescent almost-teenager. She missed her parents.

Her heroes were gone and so were their promises of great opportunity to change the world. But this change that was about to come for everyone on Earth would test even the most optimistic and could destroy the downtrodden all together. The immigration horror stories, the intolerance and injustices had just begun to slow down, slightly but noticeably. Hope had returned, following so many years of division, but it hadn't eradicated instability entirely.

Maybe that's why they were here now.

Across the room, a sea of heads twisted and turned to the television screens in the upper corner of the room. Through a chain link security box, a familiar image could be seen: the Statue of Liberty. A cacophony of shuffling filled the room as her coworkers pulled out cellphones, tablets, and computers to watch the live stream of the speech.

From the crowd, a dark man with a Latino accent shouted, "I liked it better when we were the only aliens here!"

Chuckles followed his statement.

On the television, the President of the United States appeared at the podium.

Chapter Two

KATE FOUGHT OFF the abdominal pains through a hard shift while sitting atop the corroded, iron stool that raised her height, and with it, the "authority" of her post. Like the immigrants in line, and every other worker around her, she'd been watching Ringbak Arr's speech on television. She still didn't get it, how Travs were part human and some of them were related to people on Earth. It would become instant celebrity to say that you had an alien relative, that was for sure. If there was a way for people to use this to their advantage, they'd find it.

Kate felt nothing for the Travelers. She didn't like or dislike, welcome or shun, or even really care about them. She cared about humans; these people in front of her were real, they breathed her air, filled her space, and asked for her help. She cared for them because she saw the painful uncertainty of their own futures. For Kate, the Travelers were next in line, not first.

As she looked out amongst the immigrants awaiting her rubber stamp, Ringbak talked about his hope for unity amongst humans and Travelers. That was a political stunt if she'd ever heard one. She'd seen it so many times, though it usually accompanied wealth or political influence. If you had enough money, then all you had to do was buy some real estate in the U.S. and you got a Visa to live here. *This will be no different.*

She was curious about the DNA part, a little more than she wanted to let on, even to herself, but her drifting thoughts were interrupted.

A percussive echo of three explosions rocketed through the halls of Kate's office, making the ground and walls tremble.

On the televisions, the torch on the Liberty statue burst into a disintegrating fireball, reigning sparks, ash, and molten steel down upon the crowd. The live feed went down and the screens turned to static.

Kate jumped from her desk, intuitively placing a hand on her sidearm against her hip. She ran past the long lines of immigrants who struggled to keep their place in line. She threw off her hat, sending her auburn hair flying free, and ripped off the men's jacket that imprisoned her. She bolted through the security doors and bulletproofed waiting area and out into the street, out into the noise, out into the danger.

Her boss had emerged from his office in time to see her moving away from her desk, "Stop! Agent Pierce do not go out there!" as she pushed through the door and into the street. She focused directly on the smoke-filled cluster two blocks away.

Through the panicked crowd, she zig-zagged and pushed her way through, toward the danger. *Finally.* Her reason to act was here. Her lips curled in a determined smirk as she turned into the smoke engulfing everything around her.

She slowed her pace as benches, fallen posts, and uneven ground slid under her. She could barely see a few feet in front of her with all the smog. She could hear the crackling of fire and see dim embers as she coughed on smoke.

Hundreds of Traveler supporters lay scattered along the ground, covered in blood. Broken handmade welcome signs hung from their wooden posts, still in the hands of the disoriented survivors. Blood trickled down the heads of many, others lay paralyzed with fear and pain. It was a massacre of screams for help. Arms reached up from the smoke-filled street, like a zombie apocalypse–they tried to grab her, to stop her, to get help from her. But there were too many. She couldn't help them all. She looked into their eyes, each one, as she passed and hoped they can hear her words. "Make way! Federal agent!" she shouted. "I see you... put pressure on it ... you'll be fine ... get to shelter ... someone help this man!" She hoped that someone would hear her because she was still determined to find the source of the three explosions.

"Did anyone see where the blast came from?" she shouted over and over again to any of the survivors, trying desperately to get to ground zero. She had to know who did this, but it became dreadfully obvious that she wouldn't make it that far, not in this fallen crowd and debris.

She changed tactics. Kate pushed her way through the large crowds now covering what was once the open road. She spotted a green trash bin, and with one leap she was atop it, and with a second leap she was onto a pole, scaling up toward the crosswalk signal. Pulling herself up again, she took a standing position.

She had a vantage point, an unobstructed view. And it horrified her.

Half of the people stumbled around holding their hands to their heads to keep blood out of their eyes. The cracked, giant screens showing the live feeds from Ringbak's speech were frozen on Ringbak's static face. Kate spotted another cluster of smoke, concentrated and the only sight discernible from the rest of the chaotic environment. Sirens roared. The moans of the injured tripped her up as much as the bodies on the ground did. The mixture of carnage and building debris made it difficult to identify the living from the dead. She jumped down off the pole. Anger and sadness filled her heart, but with a furrowed brow and determined lips she pressed on, into the blinding smoke ahead.

An echoing cry came from somewhere on her left, getting closer. Kate turned toward the sound and through a brief part of the sea of death she saw a young girl. She couldn't be more than six or seven years old. The girl held a welcome sign in one hand and had nothing in the other, the emptiness of her left sleeve was as painful an image as the returning abdominal pains were to Kate. The child had lost her left arm up to the shoulder, only blood and tears were left. The girl dropped to the ground and Kate knew she needed help. She wanted to run to the girl but something stopped her. Out of the corner of her eye she saw a familiar figure, the man with the military style jacket and backpack only this time the backpack lay on the ground, empty. Beside it the man knelt down, fidgeting with something. She needed to get closer but the girl, the girl needed her help.

"You! You there! Federal Agent!" she yelled toward him. She hoped, she prayed it wasn't what she thought. If he was just a man tying a shoelace then she could move on to the girl. It wasn't that. He wasn't tying a shoelace. She moved in closer as he eyeballed her, hurriedly doing whatever it was with his hands. It was a bomb.

"Help me!" the little girl screamed from behind Kate. She turned to see her water-filled eyes were fluttering, she was fading, she was in pain. Kate turned back toward the man. He was still there, doing whatever it was. She had a decision to make, a tough one. She ran toward the man. She pointed her sidearm at him, "Freeze! Federal agent! Move your hand away from the device!" the man paused but Kate knew what was coming. He pushed his hand toward an old cell phone attached to the device and a green button but before he could press it, BANG! Kate shot him dead. She ran to the bomb, it wasn't armed. She ripped away at some wires and pulled the phone away. She turned and ran back to the little girl whose cries had ended.

Kate fell to her knees. Unable to contain herself, she choked out a sob as she helplessly looked the girl over before gently lifting her into her lap and holding her. She brushed a few matted, blonde strands of hair from the child's face with a trembling hand. "I'm sorry," she eked out in between the tears and stomach pain.

The girl smiled and spoke, her voice angelic soft, and aware. "It will be alright, you look fine."

Kate smiled, full of tears and sorrow.

The girl's eyes glazed over as her body stilled and her breathing came to a shuddering stop.

Chapter Three

WITH THE SUBTLE but defined click of a switch, Kate Pierce turned the lights off. Now she could see the bright stars against the vast blackness of the night sky out her window. Memories of the little girl who lost her arm and died haunted her. But she chose to let it. She wanted to remember what she saw, she wanted to feel that pain again and lock in its memory. She had to. Without that pain, that recent horrible image, the other pains became too real and had to be managed, acknowledged, addressed. But this memory, the one of the bombing, she could use it to keep moving forward.

Soon though, the girl in her mind turned into herself as a child. Those days dancing around her tasteful yet small, cozy, leather row home with her father were the best of what she had in her memory bank. She tried to fight the encroaching thoughts but gave in and was taken away, taken back to a warmer place, a softer time when the only conflict was about which record to play next. Her father loved his vinyl, probably the only thing of value that he had, definitely the most valuable thing to Kate. Swing music, surprisingly, always won out. Her father loved it and she suspected now, as an adult, that it was because he could always get Kate to dance to it with him.

She allowed herself this moment of peace, the quiet solitude and comfort brought on by her soft side. She leaned into the wall and gently pressed her forehead against the chilled glass; it was restful, relaxing, and conducive to more of these warm memories, but they were abruptly brought to an end.

A series of sharp bangs followed by sharp pains in her abdomen caused her to wince, drop, and put one hand on her knee for stability, while the other searched for the light switch. Flicking it on, she revealed the reality of her situation. She was in a cramped, overused, and dirty bathroom, big enough to fit only her, the sink, and the toilet. After a few shakes and rattles to the side, she pulled herself out of the space and into the passenger seating area, where a woman waited for her turn inside.

Kate was aboard a moving train and made her way to her seat. Triple chimes were followed by the call out of the next stop; it was not her destination so she settled in, her own window blocked by a sleeping, fat man.

In the few weeks that had passed since the bombings and assassination attempt of Ringbak Arr, not only had the American government continued to move forward with their plans of allowing the first wave of Travelers to Earth, but Ringbak himself had been touting the importance of moving forward even in the face of potential danger to the Travelers.

Thumbing through the news feed on her smartphone, Kate was inundated with Ringbak's face, article after article. His face was everywhere. It was as if regular life had stopped and had been replaced by the Travelers, by Ringbak Arr.

Why fight it? Might as well see what's new today, she thought, swiping past story after story. She stopped on an article titled, "How to Negotiate with Aliens." It had a video link embedded. She clicked to play it and watched as Ringbak strolled onto the set of a talk show to the standing applause of the entire crowd. He shook hands with the plump but jolly British host-man, and they sat for a conversation.

Plump Man: "Mr. Ambassador, thank you for coming today, this really is special for us."

Ringbak: "It's my pleasure, I'm happy to be here."

Plump Man: "I'm glad to see you're out making the rounds. Not going to let a little thing like a terrorist attack stop you, am I right?"

Ringbak: "Absolutely, full steam ahead is, I believe, is the saying."

The man sitting next to Kate was now awake and watching the clip from over her shoulder, adding his own thoughts.

"You know they have extra alien bodies in a freezer up there and they use the parts to heal themselves. I heard that after the attacks they sent a few down to help with our wounded but they wouldn't take, too much difference in the genetics or something like that."

Kate hated these conspiracy theories. She'd been hearing them for years and they got dumber and dumber.

"Thanks, I'm good with ... all that."

The man just shrugged it off before gesturing for her to hit play.

Plump Man: "All of this news has been quite astonishing. Let me ask you, do you have a mother or father here on Earth?"

Ringbak Arr: "You know, I have some relations here, somewhere, but my priority is to the rest of the Travelers first. Once they are all reconnected, then I will focus on my own."

Plump Man: "Well, as you know, we have another guest with us here today: James Brown, the author of the highly successful book, 'How to Negotiate with Aliens,' and I'm assuming you two know each other?"

Ringbak Arr: "Yes of course, Mr. Brown is a friend to us Travelers."

Plump Man:" Let's bring him out. James, come on out here!"

Another man entered the set to mixed applause and boos. The attentive man next to Kate chimed in again, "You know I heard that he spent forty days aboard their ship torturing the Travs during those negotiations."

The man had revealed himself to Kate. The aliens were called either one of two things: "Travs" by those who were afraid that they were here to take over Earth and enslave us, and "Travelers" by those who were more accepting of their presence. Sussing someone's view on the matter fast was important these days. Like the gun debates of the early 2000's, people were divided, and admitting an opposite view usually ended in a heated argument based on conspiracy theories or cosmic enlightenment. Kate would have neither right now, she just wanted to listen.

Plump Man: "Mr. Brown, thank you so much. I want to dive right in: Was Ringbak Arr, the monument of the Travelers, a tough negotiator?"

The crowd laughed with lighthearted enthusiasm, as did Ringbak and Brown.

Mr. Brown: "I'd have to say that in my long career negotiating international trade deals, foreign government information swaps, and corporate takeovers, this was the most fun that I've ever had."

The crowd loved it, and everyone laughed, including the man next to Kate. She wasn't laughing though, and with a sigh and light groan she switched the phone off, got up, and headed back to the comfortable, quiet, disgusting, but private bathroom.

Kate knew more about the Travelers than most civilians. She was, after all, a federal employee, and it was well known on the inside that the negotiations did not go as planned. Beyond rumor was some truth, and the bulk of it relied on the same through-line; humans demanded access to the alien tech but the aliens had no access to their own tech. They had been, in all senses, on auto pilot for twenty years. To the objection of Ringbak, the U.S. Military, the first on the ship, spent days attempting to dismantle the ship, gain access to the sealed propulsion room, and even perform controlled detonations. Every time, they were stopped by impenetrable metal and uninformed Travelers who couldn't even determine how the artificial gravity worked.

Kate took one more look at herself in the bathroom mirror, just as another chime dinged. This time it was her destination: Union Station, Washington, D.C. The chimes indicated three things to Kate. First, she had to get her stuff from her seat and risk talking to the fat man again. Second, she had no idea why she'd been called down but no doubt would find out within the hour. Third, she had to find a doctor after her meeting because the pains in her stomach were getting worse.

Chapter Four

KATE ARRIVED SWIFTLY at the I.C.E. headquarters at 500 12th Street, SW in Washington D.C. where she was met by a security guard who approached her as soon as she walked in. He waved her past the long lines, security checks, and metal detectors and greeted her with nothing more than, "I will take you upstairs," which he did before opening a door and indicating with a swift motion of his hand that she was to go with him.

Upstairs was the fifty-second floor, the oldest floor in the building, the last to be renovated for sure. Kate stepped off the elevator and was greeted by the musty stink of mildewed papers and burnt coffee. The doors had old, frosted glass windows, and Kate saw the old name scrapings were still visible under the new office occupant's names. The room she was brought to had no name or number on it, but it was open and she was gestured inside.

Kate cautiously took her seat. She was one of only four people in the office and sat down in front of a bureaucratic superior behind his desk. He, along with one man in a black uniform that she didn't recognize and another man, her superior from her office, standing behind him, stared her down like she'd just personally insulted their favorite dog. Kate immediately judged the room as non-hostile though. If she was to be fired then it would have happened already–mostly likely the day after she rushed out the door and into the chaos.

She had to be here for an assignment then, but why D.C.? Her direct superior could have given her whatever assignment was to befall her. Her critical thinking became distracted by the television on the wall. They were all watching as President Umani stood again with Ringbak Arr on the lawn of the White House. Amongst them this time was not the commanders of the world like she saw at the address on Ellis Island, but instead this time they were surrounded by children.

Umani was mid-sentence when Kate took her seat. "... that is why today we are able to announce that the reattachment process has begun and is starting, as we speak, across our great nation. Children like those who you see here today, Traveler children, are being brought to their relatives here on Earth for a chance to connect with what it truly means to be human. As part of the immigration process, any child who is welcomed by their relatives is granted immediate residency with an accelerated path to citizenship."

His words made her shudder. Fast track, there it was again, the path for the privileged was faster than the deserving. Her eyes scanned the room, choosing to focus on something else, anything else. It was not a secret that she thought this whole thing was being rushed too. It was unsafe, the bombing just happened.

The superior behind the desk pulled his eyes from

the television just long enough to scout Kate's and what she was thinking.

The commander, at his ornate desk covered in trinkets from his trips around the world, on display like trophies that no one awarded, then looked at the two gentlemen standing in the back of the room. Kate easily sensed their disdain for Ringbak, maybe for the whole situation as well.

"Agent Pierce, you aren't interested in what an extraterrestrial traveler has to say? You might be the only one on Earth," he chuckled with a sarcastic grin.

"Sir, I just think we need more time to assess the threat and combat it before presenting them more targets."

"Fair enough," he agreed. "Agent Pierce, these gentlemen are from the FBI and are part of a joint task force between our two organizations. Welcome to the newly formed Reattachment and Protection Agency. The RPA is set up to bring the Traveler children under eighteen years old into the country and to their genetic relative hosts. You're being reassigned to Philadelphia."

Kate was hearing the words but not sure what they meant. Her furrowed brow gave her away.

"Is there a problem, Pierce?"

"Sir?"

"You look confused. Are the words I just said confusing?"

"The words aren't confusing but the purpose is. Sir." Did she just step in it? Go a little too far?

Her superior sighed, clearly not amused with her snark. "Look, regardless of what we all think of ..."

"Of the Travelers? Sir, I don't think they should get priority, be fast tracked while so many others wait in lines, sit in detention centers, and stand at our borders." She could see the men shift uncomfortably in their stances.

Her superior finished his thought strongly, "Regardless of what we think of the process or the Travs themselves, this is the directive, this is the purpose of this office, and you are an agent, are you not?"

"Yes, but I ..."

"And if I'm reading your file correctly," he flipped through a folder while he talked, "then it looks like you've been asking for field duty for some time now?"

"Yes, sir, but ..."

"And you must have impressed someone above all of us," he gestured around the room, "because after your stupid and dangerous, albeit probably life saving, reaction to the bombing, you're getting your wish."

"It wasn't a wish."

"Excuse me?"

He was upset and she could see it as he sat forward in his creaky chair, leaning into her as she prepared her next breath.

"I didn't wish for it, sir, I worked for it. I put in my time at the desk, I outperformed every one of my male counterparts year over year, and I put myself directly in the line of danger to assess and neutralize a threat. I didn't wish for this, I earned this."

Kate could see by the way the men straightened their postures that she had won the room.

"Be that as it may, and regardless of your views and personal opinions," that last part he said with an elevated pronunciation and disdain, "you've got a job to do now. Just be thankful."

She was thankful, even though she didn't want this

room of men to see it, she was almost giddy inside. Real field work was exciting, even if it was partially a babysitting gig.

Her boss finished it off, "Pierce, meet Agent Grace, your partner. He'll brief you on your first assignment. Now both of you, get out of my office."

"Yes, sir, and who is this?" she asked of the other agent in the room. He stepped forward, perhaps unintentionally revealing the diplomatic badge on his hip. "Dr. Lewis Marone. Nice to meet you, Agent Pierce," he said, extending his hand.

"First man Lewis Marone?"

"Yes, that's me, and I assure you this hand has been thoroughly cleaned since it shook Ambassador Arr's hand five years ago," he said with a smirk and a hint of sarcasm.

"Yes, of course." Kate rose and shook his hand.

The boss continued, "Now both of you, get out of my office."

"And Pierce," Kate turned toward him, "please don't make my life any more stressful than it is."

"Yes, sir," was the only proper response, and she delivered it.

Kate and her new partner walked out together. He was stiff and serious and he started out strong. "You and I will be assisting in the reattachment process. We will be personally delivering Traveler children to their relations here on Earth. These meetings have been pre-arranged, and the persons have been fully vetted, however ..."

"Babysitting," Pierce interrupted, directing the comment toward her new partner, hoping for a sign that he agreed. "Is this what we just signed up for?"

Agent Thompson Grace stopped her with a swift

motion of his hand. "Agent Pierce, this is no babysitting job! The terrorists are constantly tracking these children, following our every move. They will attack us as some point, Pierce, and you better be ready. And then there's the children and the ... emotions that we have to contend with." He was serious. "There is a violent organization that opposes everything that the Travelers want. We have been engaging with them during these reattachments, and they show no signs of getting any weaker, but instead are improving and advancing in their aggressive tactics."

"You've exchanged live fire?"

"Yes, and much more. They're getting more and more sophisticated with IEDs and ambushes. They can hit us anywhere along the way."

He handed Kate the folder. "Child nineteen. Female, nine years old, supposedly."

She looked down at the folder, opened it, and saw a picture of a little girl. Adorable, was her first thought. Long, blonde hair, light skin, and bright blue eyes. So many of the Travelers had bright blue or green eyes, barely a brown one in the lot.

"Sabrina."

"What?"

"Sabrina, that's her name."

"What about her parents on the ship? Doesn't she have anyone up there?"

"I don't know, it's not in the brief. But it doesn't matter, does it?"

"What do you mean?" She stopped and waited for him to turn.

"Look, Pierce, these children, they're not like, you know, normal kids."

Kate didn't think she could be more confused but somehow his statement made her wonder what the hell else she was about to find out.

"Not all the Travelers have parents up there. It's complicated, and I don't fully understand it myself but some of them appear or come out of a birthing room that the rest of them don't have access to."

"That makes no sense."

"That's what I'm saying. We don't know much about them in that way and at the end of the day, they're coming here to live with something of a real family, and more importantly there are multiple threats we have to contend with. Safety is our job, that's all."

"Multiple threats? More than the terrorists?"

"The anti-Trav groups are the ones who want to kill the children but there's another group made up of Travelers who want to kidnap these children. And believe me, they don't need explosives to be more ruthless, violent, and dangerous."

"What do we know about them?" Kate felt some excitement build within her.

"They are a small group, we have no idea where they work out of, and no one has ever seen the one in charge, but we have a name, potentially the leader: Sankeen, the most violent and dangerous of them all."

"And we expect them to hit us as well?"

"We can discuss it on the way to get the child."

Kate opened the folder and fingered through the pictures of the young alien girl. She looked cute, innocent. A couple of older folks—again, harmless-looking—were paper-clipped into the paperwork as well.

Grace was by the door. "We'll leave in the morning. In the meantime, you can work out of this office. Get to know the file, Pierce. It might save your life."

Kate sank back into the chair, pulled the folder into her lap and, before posting her heels up on the desk in front of her, she lifted the superior's uneaten Danish off the desk and stuffed it into her own mouth, an act that didn't go unnoticed by Grace.

"What? I haven't eaten anything all day," she squeaked out between bites as Grace's disapproving look vanished behind the slamming door.

Chapter Five

KATE WAS YOUNGER and much smaller than her fellow I.C.E. agents, but she had a reputation for being pretty badass. Most of the guys on her team would get hung up on her curves, her blonde hair, blue eyes. Her mother said she had the face of an angel.

The other agents left themselves wide open on the mats at the gym where they trained. She took advantage of these moments to remind them just how skilled she really was, ending in a line of broken noses, wrists, or incapacitation. She was always being underestimated. A mistake she made sure they'd never make twice.

She'd finally earned her spot in the field, on a case. Though it was where she'd always wanted to be, being strapped in a SUV with an alien child wasn't the type of assignment she ever envisioned or wanted.

She stared out the window at the line of trees blurring by. Ahead of her and behind her, matching black SUVs led and covered them through the back roads of Devon, Pennsylvania on their way to a hidden suburb outside the city. Kate had never been to this side of Philadelphia. From the reports she canvassed, the yearly horse show in Devon drew out the old money folks. From their musty mansions and into the light, they trotted around in different self-indulgent shows of pedigree. Most of the people that lived here were CEOs, real estate moguls, sports team owners, and Mayflower descendants. The file on the host family didn't point to that kind of wealth though. Still, they we upper class enough for any child to have a shot at a good life. Kate found herself wanting to make sure this child was safe, even if she didn't know her. She felt responsible now, not just as an agent, but as a human.

Kate glanced at the side passenger mirror, meeting the small, bright blue eyes of the young girl in the back seat. The girl stared out her window as well, smiling calmly, holding onto her knapsack. How could she be so happy, going to strangers?

"Sabrina, how are you doing, honey? Do you need anything?"

"No thank you, ma'am, I'm just fine."

"Are you nervous? It's okay if you are." Agent Grace looked over at Kate with, well, just a look, but Kate felt it was meant to say, "Give it a rest." Still, Kate couldn't help herself. Here was a real life extraterrestrial in the car with her. She was giddier than she expected she would be. She liked this child, she liked Sabrina.

"I'm not nervous. I guess a little, but I'm, I don't know, excited I think."

"Oh yeah, what about?"

"Well, for one thing, playing in a back yard. Do you think they have a swing set? I really want to go on a swing set, I've never even seen one in real life!"

Kate flipped open the folder on the family, thumbing through some pictures.

"Sorry, kiddo, I don't know if they do, but I bet there's a nice park nearby somewhere."

"Oh yeah! Parks! I've never been to one of those!"

Kate felt for Sabrina. She smiled at her enthusiasm. She began to tear up, and Grace noticed.

"You need a tissue?"

"No, I'm okay," Kate said, wiping her eyes.

"Remember what we talked about, Pierce."

"No, this isn't that. I'm fine." He was talking about the phenomenon whereby adults who were around Traveler children sometimes experienced overwhelming emotions. This wasn't that though. This was due to her realization that she'd called Sabrina "kiddo" just like her own father used to do to her.

The car drove past a billboard with a picture of Ringbak Arr, the leader of the Travs, the alien Travelers who were just now starting to make their way down to Earth and into society, and the president shaking hands, with the slogan, "We Can Do This!" It was a slogan that she didn't understand. It meant nothing, but people easily rallied behind it.

Grace turned the SUV off the main road and down a long, secluded driveway.

Kate kept her eyes on the trees, looking for any signs of movement or anything that appeared out of the norm. The trees parted to reveal a massive expanse of manicured lawn and pruned hedges. A few hundred yards up the long, winding drive and deep into the woods, their SUV rolled to a stop in front of the colonial style home of Jean and Robert Sutcliffe–a couple in their early fifties.

Pierce stepped out of the SUV. A door closed on

the other side and Grace came around the front to stand beside her.

"You ready for this?" he asked.

She nodded.

"Remember what we discussed, keep your eyes trained on the surroundings. Don't focus on the child, do you understand? Control your emotions or you'll lose focus, and I need you to stay sharp."

They headed up the paved steps to a wraparound porch and knocked on the white screen door.

The oak door opened to reveal a homely-looking couple. They seemed a little old to want such a young child. Mr. Sutcliffe wore overalls and a scowl while Mrs. Sutcliffe was in a pretty housecoat and an apron.

Grace took the lead with an amiable grin Kate knew was all for show. "Good afternoon, ma'am, sir. I'm agent Grace, this is agent Pierce, and we're with the Reattachment and Protection Agency. We have Sabrina with us."

Mrs. Sutcliffe picked at individual nails, going from one finger to the next as her eyes darted between Kate and Grace.

She looked like a pleasant woman, at least Kate would tell herself that. She'd tell herself anything to feel that this child would be all right.

"Oh my, she's really here?" Mrs. Sutcliffe breathed, glancing around us, most likely looking for the girl. "This is all so incredible. We could never have children of our own. I mean, not that we knew of anyway. I made cookies, you know, does she like cookies?"

Kate smiled at the woman, hoping to put her at ease. Kate looked past the side of the house to a decent-sized yard with a swing set right in the middle.

"Oh, you have a swing set! She'll be so happy." Kate tried to keep it light and friendly.

Mr. Sutcliffe grimaced though, evidently not sharing her enthusiasm. "What if we don't want to meet it?"

Mrs. Sutcliffe smacked his arm. "Nonsense, Robert, this is my blood! We're not going back on our word. We already agreed. And they brought her all the way out here. It'll be like a reunion!"

"Not *our* blood. *Yours*, not mine." He scowled at her. "Who knows what the other half is? Could be anything. Could be some Martian monster for all we know."

Mrs. Sutcliffe's cheeks pinked as she placed a hand to her chest. "That's just plain stupid. You promised. Please, give this a chance." Kate glanced back at the tinted passenger window of the SUV, where the little girl was waiting to be reunited with her human family. But Mr. Sutcliffe's reaction wasn't doing anything to ease the annoying nerves in her gut. Was she doing the right thing? Would the child be safe here? What if it was a trap and they planned on doing terrible things to the child, the kinds of things that happened that day that Ringbak Arr gave his speech? Or what if they did something less gruesome but equally cruel, where they used her, putting her on display to the world? The fame mongers in Hollywood and in the media were clamoring for an alien to put on parade, to shackle with the chains of American celebrity.

"Ma'am are you sure that you'd like to do this?" Kate asked, a part of her hoping the woman would reconsider. "It's understandable that you may have made the decision in haste, and we need to know that you won't change your mind once we leave here."

"Yes, we're sure." She nodded, ignoring the glare her husband sent her. "Please, can we see her now?"

"Of course," Grace answered and turned toward Kate, sending her off to retrieve the child.

A door opened on the SUV that was following behind them. An agent stepped out and walked to the passenger door of their SUV. He opened the door and helped the young girl out of the car. She looked cute, innocently clutching the straps of her koala bear backpack. Kate took her hand from the agent.

"Guess what? They have a swing set!"

"Are you sure?"

"Yup." Kate smiled.

Sabrina zeroed in on the Sutcliffes, her eyes widening. A grin split her face, and she broke into a run. The Sutcliffes bent down to greet her, and the little girl threw her arms around both of them, taking them by surprise. Her giggle was giddy and sent a wave of warmth through Kate's chest. Maybe she would be okay here.

Mrs. Sutcliffe dissolved into sobs, weeping as she buried her face into the little girl's curls. Mr. Sutcliffe looked away, blinking back emotions of his own, but he didn't release the girl, he was enjoying their embrace as much as his wife, it was obvious.

The warmth in Kate's chest spread throughout her, filling her with content, and she felt her lips curl into a grin as if moving on their own.

She glanced at Grace beside her as he removed his sunglasses and drew an overused handkerchief from his pocket to wipe his eyes.

A sense of panic pierced the euphoric overdose within her. She looked back at the other agents to see them overcome with the same overwhelm of emotions: smiling, laughing, or crying.

An agent was supposed to be trained to control their emotions, but these weren't her emotions, it was the side effect of being in the presence of the hybrid children when they expressed emotion. Kate was cautioned against it, but no one was ever prepared for it, this sudden rush of joy and sadness at the same time. It was not yet an emotion that humans had learned to control. It had been described to her as a new emotion, one that they'd never had before, in some ways a blend of happy and sad and everything in between.

"Our work here is done," Grace announced.

Kate and Grace walked back to their SUV as another agent stepped toward the new family to go over the details, check the house out, and explain how the reattachment would work. Climbing into the car, Kate covered her mouth with her hand as if that could hold back the onslaught of emotions. Tears trailed down her face as uncontrollable sobs wracked her body. Jesus. She hadn't cried this hard since her dad died.

The emotions coiling through her were foreign and made her feel weak and vulnerable.

She was neither of those things.

Get it together, Kate.

Agent Grace stared out the windshield, giving her a moment to collect herself.

The Travelers had been working with human scientists to understand why this happened but so far all anyone knew was that being in close proximity to a hybrid child could, and most often did, cause heavy emotions to emerge. But with enough time and practice, you could control it.

That Grace could control himself so well meant this wasn't his first time doing a reattachment or that this wasn't his first time around a Traveler child. That he wasn't a sobbing mess like she was must mean he'd done this many times before.

Grace opened the glove box and grabbed a new box of unopened tissues. "Go ahead." He nodded.

Kate reached down and ripped in.

"I was told what to expect, but I never thought ..." Kate trailed off as another wave of emotion hit her, threatening to break her down again. She took a deep breath.

"Agent Pierce, you need to understand that this emotion is not natural. It's not our choice. We aren't mourning over the loss of a loved one or reveling in a reunion with old friends. This is forced on us, every time, just like it is for every other reattachment agent. Until we know why this happens, I won't take pleasure in it for a single moment. If they can manipulate our emotions so easily, what else can they do that we have no control over?"

Kate spotted a doll on the grass where the girl had dropped it in her rush to get to her new family. She got out and bent to pick it up. It was simple, dark haired, neutral skinned, and had a button on the back. Kate pressed it but it fettered out and said nothing. She stood with it in hand, gesturing toward the house where the Sutcliffes and the girl were still standing in the doorway with the agent.

"Sabrina, you dropped this!" she called out, moving away from the car, but she was just a few steps away when the gunshots started and the bullets ricocheted off the bulletproof glass of her SUV.

"Pierce! Get down!" Grace yelled from behind her, but it was too late. The SUV parked behind theirs exploded up into the air in a mass of burning metal and landed on top of their own, trapping Agent Grace inside.

Chapter Six

KATE LANDED HARD on the ground, the doll flying from her grasp. Smoke, fire, and glass were everywhere.

Grace struggled through the smoldering metal, crawling out onto the gravel driveway.

Where was the girl?

Sabrina. That was her name.

Sabrina, not Child 19. This bomb was meant for the child and not the couple, it wasn't uncommon for the terrorists to kill Traveler children. She pulled herself up, running toward the front door of the house.

"Pierce! Where are you going?" Agent Grace yelled. "Get back here!"

Bullets shattered the front windows of the house, as shots fired from inside, narrowly missing Kate's feet. She retreated back to the mangled metal, next to a bleeding Grace who was crouched behind the mound of smoldering wreckage that was once their SUV.

"They're inside, we need to go now!" Kate demanded.

"Hold on! Get your head about you, Pierce!" He looked her over. "Are you hit? Are you hurt?"

Kate surveyed her body; there were cuts from glass and bruises from her fall but no real damage.

Kate saw blood pooling below Agent Grace. The bottom half of his shirt was soaked with blood and it made her think of the bombings, the carnage she saw. She froze. She knew there would be dangers, but this was her first field assignment and she was losing people. That's not how it was supposed to go, but she couldn't allow her emotions to control her, not now.

She met his gaze, her heart racing at the knowing look he sent her.

No.

"Grace?" she breathed.

"I want you off my property, now, or I'll kill the alien!" Mr. Sutcliffe screamed through the front door.

Kate slid aside, peering around the edge of the debris to see Mr. Sutcliffe standing by one of the windows. Behind him, Mrs. Sutcliffe was standing frozen, holding Sabrina tightly to her side, protecting her. Was he a terrorist or just one of the millions who don't want the Travelers here?

"That's not going to happen," Grace muttered and then yelled back, "Release your wife and the child, and we'll talk."

"She's not a child!" he refuted. "She's an alien invader, a plague on our soil come here to destroy us, to take us straight into hell!"

"She is still a child, don't make this mistake," Kate pleaded.

Mr. Sutcliffe, his wife, and Sabrina disappeared into the house.

"Damn it," Grace spat.

A series of rapid succession gunshots screamed out from behind Kate. She turned to see a small, armed group taking up position alongside the long driveway, just behind the trees. Three men dressed in mismatching fatigues moved closer until they were crouched down behind the smoldering SUV wreckage.

One of them yelled out, "We're here for the girl, nothing else!" He must have been talking to the agents. "Put your guns down and let us through and we'll get her."

The agents fired at the armed man behind them. The men fired back but weren't aiming at the agents, they were aiming at the tires of the last remaining SUV.

"I'm not going to say it again. Let us pass."

The agents stood to take their shots, but from across the driveway Kate could see that there were more of these militia-type men. They held their guns on the backs of the agents. "That's enough, boys, let's put 'em down." The agents did before having their hands bound together with zip ties.

Two more shots came from the house, from a busted window, and landed next to Kate. The militia men saw her now, and Grace. "You there, stay where you are!" They trained their guns on her, but seeing how they didn't shoot the agents, she thought she could make it.

Grace screamed again, with agony in every syllable, "Pierce! Move!"

She sprinted toward the house. There were no less than eight armed men searching their sights for her but only one armed man inside. Much better odds in the house.

She made it only a few steps across the soft gravel and dirt ground before another series of shots rang out from inside the house.

Kate kept moving toward the front door. She shouldered into it, barreling through like a warrior on the charge against a much larger opponent.

"Federal agent! Drop your weapon!" she shouted as she moved through the foyer, raising her gun. "Sabrina, where are you? I'm coming to you!"

Kate turned down a hall in the direction of the blown-out windows. The doors were closed.

She stopped short when she found Mr. Sutcliffe lying face down on the fine Persian rug in the middle of the living room floor. That was a fancy rug for a man like him, she thought.

He was holding the gun in a suicide pose.

Suicide? But how? Why?

Gunshots could still be heard faintly outside. Kate hoped Grace was holding up okay.

A sniffle drew Kate's attention from the body to the corner. Mrs. Sutcliffe was crying, staring at Sabrina, who stood a few feet from her, watching Kate blankly. She ran to Kate and wrapped her arms around her protector.

"Kate, I was scared!" she relayed. Kate knelt down.

"I'm so sorry, are you okay? You look okay?" She fumbled her hands around the child, scanning for wounds. Not a scratch.

Mrs. Sutcliffe stood over them. "It's all right, dear, we're fine now." She reached her hand out for Sabrina.

None of this was alright.

Sabrina looked toward Kate. Kate could feel her fear like an itch along her skin, but this time there wasn't an overwhelming surge of emotion that crumbled Kate.

"What happened here?" Kate asked lowly. "Mrs. Sutcliffe, was your husband part of a terrorist group? Is anyone else in the house?"

Mrs. Sutcliffe kept petting Sabrina's hair and rubbing her back as if Kate had not spoken.

"Mrs. Sutcliff, I need to know right now, is anyone else here?" Kate repeated evenly, keeping her finger on the trigger and ready for any surprises.

Mrs. Sutcliffe continued to ignore her presence.

"Who put the bomb under the SUV? Was it your husband? Was he acting alone? Is he with those men outside?"

Mrs. Sutcliffe's gaze drops to the floor. "He was sad. Suddenly, he started crying and he was sad and he put the gun to his own head. I felt it, I felt his sadness."

Kate glanced at Sabrina, who was watching her with a shuttered expression. She didn't know if Mr. Sutcliffe did commit suicide or if Sabrina may have had something to do with it. If she could manipulate our feelings, could she have manipulated his thoughts too?

One thing was certain, she wasn't safe here anymore.

Kate grabbed Sabrina and wrapped her arm around her. She made her way to the front door and raced back toward the wreckage, searching for Grace. It was time to go.

She ran to her partner and took in the gruesome sight of bodies lying motionless around him. Faint sirens rang out from somewhere in the distance. Too far to save anyone here.

She came around the wreckage and dropped the arm that was around Sabrina, her breath catching.

Agent Grace was lying in a pool of blood and he was fading.

"Grace!" She panicked and rushed to kneel beside him. She stopped short of touching him, afraid to move or hurt him further. She met his weary gaze.

"You're going to be okay."

The corner of his mouth barely moved. His breath hitched and he coughed, causing blood to trickle from the corner of his mouth.

Oh, god. "Just hang in there, help is on the way."

The sirens were getting closer, and she prayed he'd hold out.

"Don't." His eyes opened. His lips bearly moved as he whispered, "Protect reunion. Find Grimm. Promise."

She held his hand. "Reunion? Who's Grimm?"

"Just find him. Take the girl. Take her to him."

She knew he cared, he'd always cared for the children. He passed out, and Kate pressed her fingers to his neck, keeping an eye on his slow vitals. He was breathing shallowly. He had a pulse.

A medical team emerged quickly from out of nowhere. Kate stepped away and allowed the emergency responders to tend to her partner. She turned her attention to Sabrina.

"You did something, didn't you?" She nodded toward the house. "In there. With Mr. Sutcliffe."

Sabrina's eyes widened, and then her brows pinched. "I don't know. The man was scaring me and I got sad, real sad that he didn't want me. And then he ..." Her words trailed off as she broke down and started to cry.

Kate believed her. She picked her up and rubbed her back. "You're going to be okay. I won't let them hurt you."

Kate scanned the yard that had been so pristine and beautiful moments ago and now was a warzone of devastation.

"Sabrina, what about these other men? When we first got here, what did you do to them?" Kate asked, half expecting an answer about special alien powers.

"That wasn't me, honest. You've got to believe me, I didn't do that."

Kate scanned the yard, the driveway, the road, no sign of those men, the militia-looking ones. Where did they go?

Gunfire rang out once again. Twelve shots in the air, from different guns, then a concussion grenade exploded, the bang so loud it knocked her and Sabrina to the ground. Smoke billowed around them. Kate couldn't make out anything over the ringing in her ears and the blast of pain emanating from the back of her skull.

Her muscles seized. She heard the sound of boots scrape over the gravel. They moved around her, they seemed so close, but she couldn't grab them, not with the pain, the paralyzing pain that consumed her body. As the smoke cleared, she saw several men and women moving past her and toward the woods in the back of the house.

Where is Sabrina?

Kate worked every muscle in her body, every ounce of strength and resolve, every bit of training and determination, just to get to her knees. Sabrina was beside her, stunned but okay by the looks of her, and Kate pulled her close. She heaved the girl over her shoulder and stumbled with Sabrina's dead weight as she made her way across the yard to the side of the house. She ran her hand along it to stabilize herself as she walked, the bumps and textured siding keeping her upright and in the present.

Once around the back of the house and out of sight of the team, her knees buckled and she fell. Sabrina tumbled onto the ground beside her. Kate's abdomen pains returned with force.

She grunted, pressing a hand to her side.

She searched her body with her shaking hands, digging through the layers of clothing looking for a bullet wound, but found nothing. She was having another one of her "bouts."

God, not now, why now?

She vomited into the grass as her body was wracked with shivers.

She saw black, even with her eyes open, and soon she couldn't see anything. Violent images flooded her mind in a rush, intensifying the pain in her head.

Mr. Sutcliffe's body on the floor.

A hysterical Mrs. Sutcliffe.

Grace bleeding out.

Gunshots. The sound of each bang caused visions of Sabrina watching her. Each deafening pop played over and over again, allowing the alien to move closer into view behind Kate.

Another bang, and then another.

Sabrina's eyes grew closer and closer in Pierce's mind.

Kate had stopped vomiting, but the stomach pains turned to a white-hot fire, threatening to consume her. She screamed.

Another image hit her, this time of the little girl from the terrorist attack during Ringbak's speech. Her missing arm. Her striking blue eyes.

"Stop, stop, make it stop!" Kate pleaded.

Kate curled into a fetal position.

New images filled her head, a fetus in a womb, its heart beating, the fetus becoming a baby crying. Kate felt herself floating in thick, purple goo. She struggled to move her arms, and bubbles filled up around her. She saw the baby again, floating with its umbilical cord out in front. Her eyes followed the sight of the umbilical cord from the fetus to her own pelvic region. It was attached to her own stomach. She was naked, and her stomach was pulsating, undulating. She sank deeper into the purple goop. She saw her stomach, it was large, protruding.

What the hell?

Chapter Seven

KATE COULDN'T MOVE from where she lay in the grass. She had no idea how much time had passed. How long had she been laying here? Her eyes were heavy, and she couldn't fight the force drawing her into darkness anymore. Everything was getting blurry and darker with each shuddering breath she took.

A child's shrieking scream pierced the darkness.

Sabrina.

Her eyes went wide.

Someone was standing over her, a woman. She held Sabrina's hand and Sabrina held hers, willingly. Behind the woman was a man with a gun pointed at Kate. Kate tried to move, but couldn't. She couldn't even open her mouth to speak. If she could just reach out, she'd grab the child and pull her close, pull her to safety. But all she could do was watch this nightmare version of reality with blurred objects, silhouetted villains, and crippling fear. The woman raised her boot and pressed it across Kate's face, pinning it to the ground before releasing it. Kate worked to focus her eyes and her mind. She saw Grace, bloody, across the yard. Kate turned her sharpened eyes and attention back to the woman, the terrorist, the one who had Sabrina. She looked familiar, but Kate's blurry vision couldn't fully reconcile the face of the kidnapper.

"I know you," Kate said as the familiar woman leaned over her failing body.

"Hello, Kate. Long time no see, though I can't say I've missed you. "

Kate could feel the pain in her body giving way to coldness, numbness. She fought to keep her eyes open, grunting with every deep breath she took.

"Tendra?" she spat out, blood trailing from the corner of her quivering lips. "I don't understand."

"What don't you understand? A weak and damaged girl comes to you for help and now, well, she does this?" Tendra proudly gestured to the destruction.

"Why?"

"Why? Really?" Tendra took a breath, bent down closer to Kate, crouching over her. "The day we met, I was scared when I came to you people. I had nowhere else to go, I was begging for help and you weren't even interested."

Kate had been hurriedly finishing up paperwork at her post in the I.C.E. office. As soon as the paperwork was done, she'd had an appointment with a doctor; something in her abdomen hadn't been feeling right and she had questions

Her desk phone rang.

"Agent Pierce," she answered stoically, looking at her watch. "I've got to head out early today though." Her expression changed and irritability took over. If she was a man, they wouldn't be making her stay.

Stay calm, Kate, was her mantra.

"Okay. Bring her up." Kate folded the laptop and shuffled the papers around on her desk so that she could get back to them later.

A young woman, not more than twenty-three, walked toward the cubicle that Kate was imprisoned in. She was soft, petite, and beautiful. Her skin and hair were so perfect and her eyes were mesmerizing. The girl approached softly but with purpose as she clenched both hands to the clean handbag in front of her as it dangled and swayed above her knees as she walked. She was soft, and soft wouldn't make it in this world.

Kate motioned for Tendra to take a seat.

"Thank you for seeing me, Miss ... Pierce?" Tendra inquired, clearly nervous about the proper protocol.

"Agent Pierce," Kate amended with a tiny smile. "What can I help you with exactly?"

"My boyfriend, Kellan, and I were passing through the immigration checkpoint here when we became separated."

Kate perked up at the realization. "You're a Trav, er, I mean Traveler?"

"Yes, is that okay? Am I in the right place?"

"Sorry, yes," Kate fumbled but recovered. "You are, but I've got an appointment so I'm not sure why they sent you back to me. I don't think I can help you." Kate hated delivering that kind of a response. It made her feel like a bureaucrat, a clock puncher, but she needed to see the doctor, her bouts were getting worse.

"Why don't you tell me what happened and I'll see if I can get you to the right agent?"

Tendra's eyes revealed her appreciation. "When Kellan and I came through we were separated. They took him and put him on another boat. I don't know where he is now, he's moved, I don't know where he is, and I am scared, I'm so scared. Can you help me find him please?" She was in tears now.

Kate had to help. She picked up the phone. "I'm going to get someone for you right now." But no one answered. "Excuse me, I'll be right back." Kate stood and moved with determination toward a small office one floor below. Knocking as she entered, Stan, a pitiful-looking man behind his messy desk, looked up at her. He was not a fan of Kates, it was obvious by his change of expression upon her appearance. He had come on to her a few months ago and she'd brushed him off, and ever since he'd been a pain in the ass. Stan was the files coordinator and whenever Kate needed something, she had to go through him. It was always awkward.

"Agent Pierce, why don't you just let yourself in," he quipped.

"I've got a young girl in tears upstairs because she was pulled away from her boyfriend at immigration. What gives? Are we trying to piss them off so that they hate us now?"

"You've got a girl upstairs?" Stan leered. "Separated from her alien boyfriend, how sad. It's like a soap opera."

Kate was not standing for this. "This is not how we are supposed to be doing things around here, Stan. You need to help me out on this one."

"Look, agent, I'm the one behind the desk, I decide what records are pulled, not you."

"You're behind the desk because of your uncle's donations to the Mayor's election fund, everybody knows it."

He caved to her needs. "What're their names?"

he asked with disdain. Turning to his computer, he logged in as Kate handed him a formal-looking folder. He opened it and typed. As he read, his eyes went wide. "Oh shit."

"What is it?" Kate's brows knitted in concern.

"These aren't any ordinary aliens. Did she mention that her boyfriend is the son of their leader, Ringbak Arr?"

"No, she didn't." Kate was unsure now.

"Well, it looks like he's in Alaska and his own father requested he be sent there. That's cold. Literally. It looks like he isn't in the system anymore though. No reports on his current whereabouts. They've got a search warrant out for him. Oh wait, here it is."

"What? What is it?"

"It's classified."

"Stop it, Stan!"

"No, I'm serious, look." He turned the monitor for her to see the words CLASSIFIED across the screen.

"I'm not sure what this girl told you or what kind of game she's running, but there's no way that if she is who she says that she is, that she isn't already a part of this, whatever it is."

Kate felt tricked, used, and she was at a loss. Messy man Stan cut off her attempt to find words. "Wait a minute. Agent, you can't tell her anything. This is classified. Besides, she's playing you, Pierce. I bet she's upstairs going through your things right now," he finished with a laugh.

Kate didn't find it funny. Now she was mad at the girl and she intended to show her. Kate stormed off, angry in part by being misled but angrier about missing her doctor's appointment.

Back at her desk, Pierce fired off a glare that pushed Tendra back. Kate scanned the desk, looking for signs that her stuff had been messed with. She saw her drawer was slightly open. It could be a coincidence, but Kate wasn't taking the chance. She slammed it shut.

"I can't help you, and you need to leave."

Tendra looked shocked. "Why? What did I do, what happened?" she asked as she stood uncomfortably.

"I'm not here to be played. You'll have to find help somewhere else. I'm sure it's not as hard for you and your boyfriend as the others, is it?"

Understanding flickered in Tendra's eyes. She held her shoulders high, leaving the office and Kate's death stare.

Now, Kate stared up at the young, girl though she didn't look that young anymore. She looked worn, tough with her tactical clothes and pulled back hair. Her shoulders were broad, and her tank top revealed a muscular torso.

"That's why you're doing this? You're kidnapping children because I wouldn't help you find your boyfriend four years ago?"

"No, you're just not worth that much to me, Kate–I mean Agent Pierce," she said sarcastically. "I'm not a terrorist, Kate, you are. I'm a savior."

"Ha, savior? From what?"

"Do you even know what really happens to these children after you leave them behind? You think they all go on to live happy, little lives, just like the human kids around them? Well they don't. They get snatched back up a few days after being dropped off. Your government makes claims that there is some final DNA testing that needs to be done but that's not what happens at all. They get taken, hauled off and experimented on, over and over again until they're shells of what they were. Then and only then are they dropped back off to their human families to live out their time here broken, fractured, and beaten."

"There's no way. We would never do that!" Kate stopped short when Tendra drew closer, revealing a hand-carved knife that resembled a large animal claw fashioned into a dagger. Tendra took the knife and used it to slowly lift Kate's shirt, revealing her stomach.

"You, Agent Pierce, are *not* in the know." Tendra pricked at a minuscule scar, making Kate wince. "Do you know what that is? The little crescent scar?"

"It's nothing, a scar from climbing a tree when I was a kid. What does that have to do with you being a terrorist!?"

"It's not from rock climbing. It's from where they took your child. The one that was brought to my ship and raised as one of us."

Kate didn't have a child. She'd know. "You're lying."

"Am I? Are any other agents being told they have Trav kids? I bet not. Why weren't you told? Why aren't you being reunited? Why are they keeping agents from their offspring?"

"Because I don't have a child."

"I wonder what they're doing to her right now?"

Tendra stood and wiped the dirt off her pants.

"Find your child, Kate. You'll see. And when you do, when you have your answers, you'll join me."

"That ... will ... never ... happen," is all that Kate could expel before her mouth was met by Tendra's foot, knocking her out cold.

Chapter Eight

AGENT KATE PIERCE handled her badge, fidgeting with it. She eyeballed it and ran her finger over the gold lines before tucking it into her pocket. She stood, falling intentionally off the examination table enough to get her feet to the floor. Kate changed back into her clothes, dropping the gown that the nurses gave her faster than she slid off the table. She secured her gun in its holster and pulled her RPA windbreaker on. She exited the confines of a doctor's examination room, and entered the active, busy hallway. Nervously scanning the halls, she felt eyeballs on her–all of them. Thinking she was being paranoid, she straightened up and walked on. She found her way to the end of the hall and to the formal doctor's office she was meant to be in. Kate entered the office and took her seat in the comfortable chair across from the grim reaper.

"How bad is it?" she demanded with the subtly of a scared child.

"Your injuries from the attack are minor, nothing really to be concerned about, though you'll have that shiner for a bit longer."

"That's great, thanks doc." Kate stood to leave,

ready to charge out into the world and get back to the business at hand–finding Sabrina.

"Not so fast, Agent Pierce."

Ugh. She hated these government doctors. When they said "agent," they meant "subordinate."

"Is there something else?" Kate sat back down into the springy but dated office chair.

"I reviewed your medical history and spoke with your doctor before examining you. I know the tests were uncomfortable for you, invasive even, but they raised some real questions."

Kate felt nervous now. She worried that the pains, the flashes, and the scar that indicated something more was wrong with her, but she felt fine–today anyway–and she wanted to get out of this office and out of this pattern of thought. She wanted to focus on one thing: Sabrina.

"Kate, I have to ask you something, and I'm sorry if it's personal, but–"

"What is it? You can ask." Kate took some control of the conversation, that was something.

"Did you have an abortion?"

"What? No. Never. In fact, just the opposite. I've been told that I can't have children."

"Yes, I know, I saw that, but–"

"What? What is it?"

"I'm sorry that I have to put you in this position, but it certainly explains the pains you experienced. I know I haven't examined you before but none of your previous records indicated the procedure, but given the significant trauma to your uterus and ..."

"When?" is the only word that Kate could muster. It's a question she didn't want ask but needed answered.

"Excuse me?" The doctor seemed startled.

"When did it happen? When was the abortion?"

"I was hoping that you could tell me because it doesn't appear to be recent."

"When!" she demanded before composing herself. *Come on, Kate, be strong,* she thought before continuing, "If you had to estimate, could you say when?"

"Maybe five to six years ago? I don't, I mean it's not something I can really tell just by looking, but from what I've seen in other similar patients and the scarring ..."

"Oh my god," Kate cried, allowing herself the emotion that she planned for, but didn't expect to arrive in this way. "Oh my god."

"Kate, can you tell me where you had it done? There are repercussions to this ... this, malpractice. I may be able to track down some records and ..."

"It didn't happen. I never had one. I told you that already!" Kate felt hysterical. But she couldn't give in. She was not the woman who cried in her doctor's office. But her composure was gone. She wanted to hold onto the rationalization that this made no sense, but that wasn't true. She felt it: the tingling in the back of her neck, alerting her to a puzzle that needed to be solved. Her mind raced, so deep were her thoughts and memory flashes that she couldn't hear a word the doctor said. He just droned on, and her mind was on fire. The ship, the explosion, the speech, Ringbak, immigrants, attachment, hybrids ... hybrids. How did they become hybrids? Ringbak's words that day: "Your stories of UFOs and abductions." Why would he say that unless ... unless he knew this would be the effect on the women who were taken. Kate saw it all now. She would have had the same reaction had she known, had she suspected, had she remembered. Pain grew and anger festered inside her. Rage, uncertainty, more pain, then nothing, nothing but an image inside her mind. A child. Sabrina? Too old for what she was thinking but ... somewhere, up there, she had a child, a five- or six-year-old.

Just like all the other women who were being reunited with their children, she was one of them. She had a baby. But the timing didn't make sense, it was confusing to her—as it was to everyone. How could they be on a ship for twenty years but have hybrid children who were under ten?

"Kate, maybe we should talk about this, figure out what to do next." His words were clear now, like a starting pistol.

"What to do next?" Kate was on her feet; she was on fire. "They took my baby and I'm going to get it back, that's what to do next, that's the only thing to do next." She stormed out, her purpose replacing pain, her focus replacing hysteria, her speed replacing emotion.

Kate stared down the elevator numbers as her car rose steadily toward floor 52. The last time she was here she had been reassigned. Now she was about to brief her superiors on the attack that took Agent Grace's life. She wondered if the other people in the small space could tell how angry she was. She anticipated a confrontation during the debrief, where she'd accuse them of withholding information about her own child. Maybe they knew about the source of her "bouts" all along, maybe they had her child. She tried to separate her anger from the hypothetical. Storming in there and making demands wouldn't work. These were federal officers at a commanding level she'd be dealing with; they never gave in to pressure. It was part of their job. Kate swallowed her breath. *Think, think, what do I know?* She gathered her thoughts, breathed deeply to calm her heart rate, closed her eyes, and waited for an answer to come. It didn't, but an idea did. She had a plan and noticed that it made her calmer. When she opened her eyes, she had arrived at floor 52.

At the end of the large room, across the bullpen, was the office she was meant to be in. But closer to her, the nearest office, was the important one: the Records Coordinator's Office. She looked at her watch. *I have time.*

The records coordinator was a woman. *Flirting is out then,* she thought. This would be so much easier if it was Stan, but he was still going to help even if he had no idea.

She knocked and entered.

"Can I help you?" the older woman asked as she peered at Kate with a tilted chin and from above her bifocal glasses.

"Hi, sorry, I'm not sure if you're the right person I'm supposed to tell, but I was told there's an error with the records database system downstairs and the IT guys are about to reboot the system without you?" Kate had no idea if that would work but she recalled hearing a similar thing happening at her own office and it sent Stan running out the door screaming, "Stop, stop!"

"Hmm," the aging woman replied. "This again. Well thank you for alerting me," she said calmly before she got up and left. Kate smiled as she walked by, and when the woman disappeared around the corner, Kate went in.

She sat at the woman's terminal. She knew she couldn't log in with her own credentials–her clearance was too low. But Stan's wasn't. His would work, if he hadn't changed his passcode. She had seen him punch it in so many times with his slow, stubby fingers. She logged in without an issue, but she knew it might have logged him out at his own terminal, so she had to move fast.

First query, "Kate Pierce," yielded over two hundred results; too many.

Combined search "Kate Pierce" and "Traveler child." Nothing. What was it Grace had said? Reunion.

Next query, "Reunion." Results: sub-database access required. *Okay, never saw that before.*

New inquiry within the sub database, "Kate Pierce, child" ... INSUFFICIENT INFORMATION.

Maybe "Sabrina?" It was a longshot ... INSUFFICIENT INFORMATION. What did that mean?

Maybe just "Kate Pierce" ... INSUFFICIENT INFORMATION. Ugh. What about Kellan and Tendra?

New query, "Kellan Arr" ... DECEASED. KIA. What, that made no sense; killed in action?

New query, "Tendra Shadestone" ... WHEREABOUTS UNKNOWN. Huh ... this wasn't getting her anywhere. Kate stared at the query search box. It blinked at her like a hand waving her in. *Come on, Kate, come on ... think!* Grimm. Grace said to find Grimm.

New query, "Grimm" ... Three results: 1. Charles Grimm, Philadelphia, Pennsylvania address search. 2. Asset Category: Missing Persons/ Remote Viewing. 3. Project Reunion, Stage 4. Kate was overwhelmed with options even though there were only three. Each one was their own potential rabbit hole, except for the address, so she clicked that one first and jotted it down on a piece of sticky paper before she tucked it away in her pocket. Next, Project Reunion. She clicked but nothing happened. She clicked again and nothing happened. On the third click the system shut down.

Shit! she thought just before the door was kicked open.

"Agent Pierce! Move away from the terminal!" the unknown man with the pointed gun barked while the aging librarian woman watched from afar.

"Okay, okay!" Kate raised her hands, stood up, and took a few steps away.

"That won't be necessary, agent," another man, her superior, indicated.

"Yes, sir." The agent obliged, holstering his sidearm and walking away.

"Sir, I was just–"

"Okay, save it, Pierce. Let's go, it's time for your debrief."

He was calm, and she was surprised. Why wasn't she in cuffs right now? If this wasn't that important to him then he must really need to hear what she had to say about the attack.

"Have a seat," the superior offered her, and she did. The office was exactly how it had looked before–the same dingy atmosphere, the same smell, the same dusty knickknacks. Mostly the same, except Agent Grace wasn't there. It was just the two of them. No one else was in the room. There wasn't a camera or a recorder or two-way glass. Kate knew immediately that this was not an official debrief.

"Agent Pierce," he said with a file in his hand, "let me make one thing perfectly clear. We do not know if you have a Traveler child. I'm not saying that you don't, but just that we don't know and that's intentional."

Kate felt a sinking feeling growing inside. She'd just learned two very important facts. She may have a child and the agency was purposely keeping her from knowing.

"Sir, I don't understand. Are you saying that I may have a child out there and you are stopping me from finding out?"

"Not me, Agent Pierce–them," he said while pointing above. She knew who he meant: the Travelers, Ringbak Arr. He continued, "When we agreed to this program of uniting alien children with human parents, a lot of consideration had to go into how to manage this properly. Ambassador Arr thought it most important that agents involved in the reattachment not be made aware of their own potential offspring as it may sway their loyalties toward more or less sympathetic causes."

"You mean we might become terrorists, like the one who kidnapped Sabrina. Why would you ever agree to such a thing, why would we as an agency agree?"

"It was non-negotiable. I'm sorry."

"Then I quit." Kate was sure she could game her way out.

"I see. Well, what about Child 19, Sabrina? What about Agent Grace? You're going to quit on her and let his death mean nothing?" He had her, and he knew it. That's why he'd told her everything–he knew she would never give up on Sabrina.

"We need you to find her. We need you to find them both."

"Sankeen."

"Yes," he confirmed. "We haven't been able to figure out who she was, or if she is even a she for that matter, but now it's clear from your report that she needs to be stopped. I understand you've met her before?"

"Yes. Once. She came in looking for her boyfriend, Kellan, only back then she wasn't Sankeen the Bloody, she was Tendra Shadestone."

"Well, you may be the only one in the entire agency to ever have spoken with her so that makes you the lead on this one."

"Sir?" She wasn't sure she'd heard him right, but he was standing, ready for her to leave.

"That's right. Congratulations, Pierce, you're in charge of this one. Be back here on Monday morning, and we'll get your team together. Now go try to rest this weekend, will you?"

"Yes, sir." She had a little smile, she knew it showed, but she was happy, to lead, to find Sabrina, to stop Tendra.

"And one more thing: stop breaking into federal databases, will you? It'll just cause more headaches for me."

"Yes, sir."

Chapter Nine

THE RITTENHOUSE SQUARE neighborhood of Philadelphia was an "upper crust" existence in the midst of a metropolitan center. Akin to Manhattan's Park Avenue, it defined the dance between celebrity athletes and old-world money that was the wealth of the city. Kate walked through the park at the center of the square where dog walkers and nannies relaxed under the blanket of protection that a wealthy place like this warranted. Absent were the police that Kate would see while jogging through Central Park. They didn't need police here, they were safe here, they were rich here. Were these people, the ones watching other people's children and pets, aware that they lay alongside Antoine-Louis Barye, Buck Manship, and Albert Laessle whose statues decorated this tiny patch of grass, she wondered. Probably not. It was a small park, and Kate was at its end and the completion of her pondering.

Amidst the high-rise luxury and nestled between the boutiques and brasseries was a house. It was a large house for any city street. It was old, maybe it belonged to a Mayflower family. It had that old-world detail on its face, but it was not overwhelming, in fact, it sat perfectly still, a romantic and picturesque brownstone mixed up within this neon world.

This was the address, Kate realized as she tucked the scribbled paper away in her shirt pocket. Strangely, she pondered, there was no doorbell but instead a door knocker. *Who doesn't have a doorbell, let alone a camera on their front door, especially in the city?* Wealthy people, it seemed. This knocker was surrounded by class. It was ostentatious considering the solid oak farm door on which it rested. The head of a lion eating a snake, wrapped in gold stared at her from a distance of no less than a foot. She lifted then dropped the weighted knocker, and the momentary metal on wood thud was eclipsed by an alarming symphony recognizable as church organs playing the theme song of Andrew Lloyd Webber's "Phantom of the Opera."

Kate realized that all the class and sophistication that history grounded here had officially left the square and she immediately regretted standing there holding its bags.

The woman who opened the door looked like she'd lost a fight with her lipstick and blush, but her smile was infectious. This was where Grace wanted her to go? It wasn't making sense. She'd swiped the address so quickly, maybe she'd gotten it wrong. But no, the system did reveal a missing person's agent lived here so that part made sense. But then again, it came with that extra bit of info: the remote viewing program. She had heard the rumors that the bureau had "psychics" that they used to help find missing people. Could that be what this was about? She didn't have the luxury to wonder, a little girl's life was on the line and if this guy could help, she rationalized, then she would pursue this option.

"Hello, I'm Agent Pierce from the RPA," she announced while brandishing her scuffed badge. Usually when a person heard the word "agent" they retreated and mentally paused to think about all the lies they'd ever told or petty suburban crimes they may have committed. Most people here would slam the door and tell the feds to find their lawyer. The woman staring back at Kate didn't even consider it.

"Oh! Honey, it looks like your badge has seen some days, let me tell you, I can feel that pain. We the same, you and I, battle tested and no worse for the wear, you know!"

Kate didn't know, she had no idea what this woman was saying in her creole accent, but next to the door was a table with tarot cards and a crystal ball. Kate, like most in law enforcement saw tarot card readers as charlatan grifters, gypsies who preyed on little, old ladies. Still, she persisted, "Ma'am I was told that this was the address of someone who helps the FBI with missing person's cases. Does that sound familiar to you?"

"Oh yeah, child, let me tell you, he find whoever you need, you just ask that's all, don't pay the rest no mind, he get you all sorted, you got a picture with ya, do ya?"

Kate was taken aback by the woman's enthusiasm and hospitality on the matter, and before she could answer, a tall, slender, dark man appeared from the shadows of the dimly lit house.

"Lights please, Matilda," the man commanded with an eccentric flare and a hand wave, as if orchestrating a scene in a play. Kate looked to the woman but she didn't move except to catch Kate's eye.

"Honey, I ain't Matilda, and Matilda ain't no fool. She know better than to be commanded, I tell ya."

The man tried again. "Matilda, hello, good morning. If you'd please, would you mind sharing some light with us so that this young woman might be allowed to take in the splendor of our humble abode?" This man was quirky, he overemphasized every third word or so. *If you'd* pleeease and *this young woooooman.*

Kate thought to herself, Who's he talking to, first of all, and secondly, he's dressed in a purple velour suit with a blue ascot and gold glasses. Before she could wonder aloud, the lights come up with it an apology from Matilda.

"Sorry for the delay, Magnificent. Are the current illumination levels to your liking?" Matilda was a computer coming through a speaker within the house, and she'd turned up the lights to an exceptionally high level, startling the man she called Magnificent, but revealing that beyond his tall and lanky body was a palace even larger than it seemed from the outside, complete with a working fountain in the center standing below a monstrous basket of plants and flowers and– Kate couldn't believe it–doves perched within.

"Wait, I know you, you're ..." Kate wanted to reveal his identity before he could but he'd clearly played this game before.

"Magnificent Grimm, Magnificent Grimm, you overpriced dishwasher!"

"Excuse me?" Kate retorted.

"Sorry, not you, Matilda. She's just playing with me, I know it. Sorry, I am ..."

"The Magnificent Grimm. I know, I've seen you perform."

"Well I do love to put on a show for the men and women in uniform, is that why you've come? No wait, it's something else, don't tell me. Ah yes, well sadly I cannot accommodate that request, my dear, as I am married to my work." His smirk was as off putting as it was charming. How did she not put two and two together? This man was a mentalist, a magician, a performer, but why him?

"What? No, I'm not, I mean, listen, my partner sent me to find you, he's in a coma and ..."

"Ah, voices from beyond, one of the great mysteries of the universe: can we communicate with the dead? Excellent question and I'm sure Ms. Wezlier can help you unravel that mystery as I must prepare for what may or may not be a troubling day." He smiled, stepping in close to her. "We'll just have to read the cards, I guess. Great to see you, thank you for coming by."

Kate hardly realized that at some point he had taken her by the hand and lead her back to the front door. She felt herself wake up and she was out on the front stoop. She turned back toward the door and pounded on it.

"No, stop! That's not what this is about. My partner, Tom Grace, sent me to you. It's about a missing girl." The door opened.

"Ah, how is Agent Grace? Is he ... improving?" Kate hated the way he said that, "improving," as disingenuous as the man saying it. This guy was not going to be any help, she realized. He was a clown, a side show performer who Kate had seen perform at both a Las Vegas nightclub and on the football field of her alma matter. All that was here was a parlor trick magician. Still, she couldn't shake the feeling, the nagging. Why did Grace want her to come see this man? If there was any chance he could help, then, she thought to herself, *I have to push.*

The rhythmless hum of an unplaceable tune fell clumsily from the lips of Ms. Wezlier as she cooked something delightful-smelling in the kitchen.

"Do you have the target image?" the man insisted with authority.

Still trying to make sense of things, Kate insisted in return, "I'm sorry, what are you exactly? Are you a profiler or something? Do you use your tricks to help find missing children?"

The man paused, placing four of his five fingers to his head in mock shame. He removed his golden glasses as he exhaled. He obviously saw her as nothing more than a draw on his time. Nevertheless, he agreed to answer her inquiry.

"I am a man with a well-developed skill and experienced ability which allows me to locate people, places, and objects, under the right circumstances, which are generally unfindable by others, unless of course they already know the location of the person, place, or object or in the rare case where they possess the same skill and ability as me." Before Kate could process the words, he continued, "Now, can we get started please? I feel your negative energy just filling my beautiful home, and I'm afraid the doves have already starting to fall ill just due to your mere presence." He looked up at her from his hand which now cradled a baby dove.

"Your vibe is literally killing my plants." He gestured up to the hanging basket as now-wilted leaves fell from it.

"How did you ...?" Kate was confused again, and could only tell that she was walking by the fact that she could see her own feet moving below her though she couldn't control where they were going.

Kate found the energy to answer, still unsure of where she was or what was going on.

"Yes, sorry, but who ..."

The man cut her off, "Thanks again for coming, take a moment before driving, will you?"

Kate heard those words but they don't register in time to stop the golden, serpent-eating lion from stopping short of her nose as it slammed. The sound jolted her into the reality that she was standing back out in the street, again. She felt confused, disoriented.

Oh that's it! She'd seen him hypnotize people in the crowds! He was a hypnotist, that's what he'd done to her! She stuck her foot into the door before it could shut.

"It's a little girl! Please!"

He opened the door again and gestured her in. His smile had disappeared and a serious man stood before her.

"Follow me." He turned and walked away, and she followed quickly as he headed down a basement stairwell.

"Target information please? Who are you looking for?" Entering before her, he revealed a dark and empty room consisting of nothing but two chairs. One was positioned alongside the wall. He motioned for Kate to sit in a basic folding chair. The other chair resembled one you'd find in a dentist or barber shop and it sat in the middle of the room, secured to the floor by its large, round, metal base.

Kate did the best that she could to answer his question. "The target is a child, nine years old, blonde hair, long blonde hair, blue eyes, umm ..." She faltered for a moment, realizing that she didn't really know much, but there was something distinguishing. "She's a Traveler child."

And with that, the peculiar, rude, and domineering, pain-in-the-ass of a man stopped. Once standing tall, he appeared slimmer and less broad now, hunched over for a moment when he turned back toward Kate. She knew the look on his face, she'd been reading it on the faces of hundreds recently: fear.

"You mean this target is a hybrid?"

Kate was surprised by the question, especially from a psychic, but he didn't allow her to answer. Instead, he continued, "Miss Pierce, I am a remote viewer. I am not a mystic, a psychic, or a medium. I am able to concentrate and focus in order to give a best guess as to where someone might be. But Traveler children, they ... they ... I can't ever really place them. It's like they don't live here, or anywhere, for that matter. I can't explain it, but I can never see them. I'm sorry you've wasted your time coming here, I really can't help you."

And with that, he had led Kate straight through the room and to a back door. It wasn't until he opened it, revealing the cold night, that Kate realized he was kicking her out again.

She protested, "Please you've got to help me, I need someone to help me and whatever your unusual ability is, maybe it can help me, help that little girl. She's alone. Can you imagine, I mean really imagine what it would be like to be nine years old and not have any family, only to find one and then to be violently ripped away from it?" Kate wiped a few tears from her eyes.

The man stopped, he looked to be considering it for a moment, and Kate looked deep into his eyes and felt something, sympathy maybe, she wasn't sure what it was, but she knew he was going to help.

"Can I ask you something, Agent Pierce?"

"Yes, of course, I should have a picture here somewhere." Kate fumbled through her tears and her pockets.

"No." He stopped her. "Not that."

"What then? What do you need to know?"

"Why do you believe her to be your daughter?" Kate didn't expect that. She gasped for breath, not sure how to answer.

"Never mind. I know the importance of time in these situations. I will help you, please sit. Now."

The man took a seat on his barber-dentist chair, removing his golden glasses and wiping the lenses clean before settling back down and continuing, "Do you have a picture of her?"

Kate responded quickly, "Yes!" Pulling out her phone, she found a picture and showed him. He looked at it briefly and then asked her to leave it.

"Place it on the floor beside me then sit down and please don't say a word until I'm back."

Kate smelled a rat. "Wait, back? Where are you going, you just ..."

But he cut her off, "It's a figure of speech. Now sit. Please."

Kate watched silently as the man settled in and closed his eyes. A few heavy breaths and then a sigh. She saw something, but wasn't sure, and leaned in just a bit so that she could focus on his glasses, and as she watched, they fogged up in front of her eyes. Obviously an effect from heat and cold. It was drafty down here, and it was raining outside. Perhaps humidity? She couldn't be sure, and like the trick he'd pulled getting her outside, she felt inclined to doubt anything she witnessed. Nevertheless, his glasses were fogged up and remained that way as he lay back in the odd chair.

Kate must have checked her smartwatch three or four times already, but she checked it again anyway. This time, ninety-eight minutes had gone by and still nothing. She wondered if foggy-glasses-man was just asleep. Maybe it was his process. She couldn't ask and risk getting tossed out again so she decided on a rest. She closed her eyes, and sleep attacked her like a ninja pouncing from the shadows. She went out.

Chapter Ten

A STILL IMAGE hovered in the black void, out of reach but attainable at the same time as if it was calling to her. It floated close and far, like it was attached to a wave, first coming then drawing back. A swift jump and she was upon it, but it took on shape, dimension. It was an image of a car accident but it was entirely in front of her. She kept moving forward, toward the rear of the image, a mangled car, a black SUV. Chards of broken glass flanked either side, everything was frozen—sort of.

The sound of clanking and scraping metal mixed with glass breaking, but it felt distant, miles away, even though the images were right in front of her. She moved past them too. She was inside the wreck as it was happening. A blast, some fire, then another right in front of her. She fell fast into a black nothingness.

Ahead, again, there was something. A wire framed image like you'd see in a blueprint but three dimensional. And suddenly red was all around her now. It was a frame of a house. A man spoke unknowable words, but they were words, a human language. She heard it, he heard it.

Grimm was inside the house with her but didn't see her. They heard a child's voice, she was laughing. He moved closer, and she followed him. The old frame disappeared and a new one constructed itself in front of them, this time there was wallpaper instead of black emptiness. There was a floral pattern, old, looked musty. Then the girl, on the floor, it was Sabrina; Kate saw her surrounded by other children and adults, they were enjoying her, they were all laughing together. But it all suddenly stopped, the adults froze, and so did the girl, holding a doll in one hand and using the other that had been previously caressing the doll's hair, to raise it high above her head, feeling the air like you'd do while sticking your hand out the car window while driving.

She moved it toward Kate, and Grimm and said, "What are you doing here?"

A rumbling sound took over. Everyone disappeared except Kate. Even Grimm was gone, and Kate stood alone in the room. The rumbling grew louder, and water pooled at her feet. She tried to move but was stuck. A tidal wave of water came in through the windows, the door, the cracks in the ceiling, and flooded her until she was underwater, unable to move or breathe.

Kate felt something on her shoulder and looked to see it was a hook, a massive fishing hook lodged into her armpit and it was yanking on her, eventually pulling her up and out of the water.

Kate awoke rapidly. She tried to catch her breath but spasmed off the folding chair and onto the floor. Grimm stood above her.

"Where are we? What happened? What was that?" She searched the room frantically, her eyes darting back and forth. She looked around but everything was gone, she was back in the basement, with Grimm, dry.

"That's the first time someone's followed me in, Agent Pierce. I wouldn't recommend you do it again."

"How did I do that?"

"It's actually not that complicated, but forget about that. I have it."

"You know where she is? You have an address?" Kate clumsily inquired as she pushed the hair from her mouth and struggled to adjust her eyes to the light.

He continued, uninterrupted by her confusion, "I told you that there is something wrong about those children."

"What did you get?!"

"Take this and leave, please," he asserted while handing her a torn piece of yellow notepad paper.

Kate looked it over. "This isn't an address, what am I supposed to do with this?" she protested.

First a sigh, then a wipe of his glasses, and then an answer, as if it was a waste of his time. "I've described a very specific arrangement of trees, weeping willow, along a path leading up to a colonial farm house. Weeping willow trees grow eight feet per year, there are eleven of them here, and they are no taller than ten feet which means that they are young and newly planted. I'm sure the extensive resources of the federal government can locate who purchased eleven weeping willow trees in the last year."

Kate looked at him. He was right, this would be easy.

"Now, please go," he demanded softly. And with that, she was gone, still preoccupied with thoughts of these strange occurrences. But they'd garnered the clue she now held in her hand, a real clue, a real lead.

But what did he do to her mind in the beginning, how did she get outside? Like the emotions that swelled during the hybrid children's presence, she worried about how open her mind was to outside influence. Before she left, he added a parting shot.

"There's someone else, Agent Pierce." He had Kate's attention; she turned to listen.

"There's a girl. I'm not sure why, but her shadow covers the child. She's protecting her from something or someone." Kate knew who he meant, Tendra or Sankeen the Bloody. Kate saw her too and what was even more confusing was that Sabrina was holding onto her and they both looked happy.

Chapter Eleven

FOR THE THIRD time in just as many weeks Kate once again found herself in the RPA headquarters. Her trip to Philadelphia had been short but fruitful. A tactical meeting was scheduled for early Monday morning and she hoped it meant that the description that Grimm provided had yielded a valuable result.

The briefing room was filled with armed agents, tactical gear, and weapons. Kate looked around at room full of strangers. She didn't know any of them but she could tell by the way they interacted, smiled, joked, and talked that they knew each other.

A bearded and buff agent raised a detached sight to his eye and peered through it before commenting to the similar-looking agent next to him, "We'll get the kid, but I want to make sure we don't miss the target."

"I hope she doesn't plan to use the kid as a human shield," the other one remarked.

"Yeah, I hate when they do that, but it is what it is."

"Sabrina," Pierce interrupted.

"Excuse me?" one of them said.

"Her name is Sabrina."

"Yeah right, Sabrina, we know. We didn't mean—"

"Good, just keep that in mind when you've got your finger on the trigger because if she so much as gets a scratch on her wrist from any of you, I'll be the first one testifying at your criminal hearing."

"Excuse me?"

"You heard me. I'll make sure you are stripped down and brought up on charges. Do you understand?"

"Yes, ma'am," they both responded in unison. Kate was fierce, they had to know, well she hoped they did at least. She turned from them and took a deep breath. That was hard. She meant it and she felt it but she wasn't used to reprimanding heavily armed agents, especially men that were twice her size.

The director entered the briefing room, and everyone turned toward him. James Clarke was a big man, bigger and stronger than any of the buff agents or soldiers in the room. He stood taller than everyone too, much taller. Kate knew of his work at the agency, his record of successful reattachments spoke for itself, but the wannabe jocks in the room worshipped him for his college football record and his recent induction into the Hall of Fame. He commanded any room when he spoke.

"Listen up. Based on newly acquired information, we've got a high-probability target site, and an assault and extraction plan has been worked out. Agent Pierce will be the lead on tomorrow's mission, but you'll all be following the plan put together by former agent, Grimm Maro. Come on up please." He motioned to Grimm. Kate couldn't believe it. The magician took his place next to her boss, standing almost as tall as him, but gone were the gold glasses and funny suit and in its place was the tactical gear of a seasoned agent.

"Agent Pierce and I have identified a farmhouse in Hagerstown, Maryland up near the Pennsylvania border. It's about a ninety-minute drive so I'm going to make this quick so we can get on the road. Lights please." The lights went down and a project fired up and satellite imagery appeared showing a farmhouse in a rural area. As it moved in closer, a long road became more defined, and Kate saw two rows of weeping willow trees.

He was right, Kate thought. They found it. But why was he here? What value did he bring now and why did it feel like he was really the one in charge?

Grimm ran through a few more details before wrapping it up and ordering everyone to gear up and fall into their vehicles. Then he and Director Clark approached Kate.

"Agent Pierce, I believe you know Former Agent Maro." He wasn't asking, he was condemning, although he was so tall that anything that he said would make her feel like he was talking down to her.

"Yes, sir, we met—"

"Next time, agent, when you have a potentially relevant lead regarding an ongoing investigation you will bring it to me first before looking into it on your own. Understood?"

"Yes, sir." She strengthened her stance and stood with her arms behind her back like a cadet.

"Very well," he said. "Good luck today. Save that little girl, will you? Save Sabrina."

Chapter Twelve

SANKEEN BRUSHED THE hair away from Sabrina's eyes. Showing her gentle compassion as she tucked the young girl into bed, she had the care of a young mother even though this wasn't her child.

"Sleep well tonight, and remember that I'll never let anything bad happen to you, ever."

"I know," the young girl replied with quiet yet comforting confidence. "I feel safe with you, Tendra, I always have. We all do. Thank you for bringing me here, I missed everyone from the nursery. Do you think we'll always be able to see each other, me and the rest of the kids?"

Sankeen looked out across the room full of young children ranging in age from five to twelve. Nearly a dozen of them were tucked away in their own beds, together in a curtain-lined room, partitioned away from something else.

"If I have anything to say about it, then yes." She smiled at the tucked in girl.

"I miss Kellan." Sabrina's eyes were downcast.

"Me too."

"Do you think about him?"

"Every single day." That was true, she never stopped thinking about him no matter how much had changed around her, no matter how much had changed inside of her.

Daniel joined them both and sat next to Tendra. He placed a soft but well-intentioned kiss onto her lips. She smiled and returned the affection, placing her hand upon his cheek, revealing their relationship.

"Hey there, Sabrina, are you doing okay tonight? Ready for some sleep?"

"Yes, Daniel, thank you. We were just talking—"

Tendra cut her off, "Sabrina was asking about the name Sankeen and where it came from."

"It sounds so beautiful, what does it mean?" Sabrina inquired with a drowsy dizziness that appeared just before sleep. Tendra returned her gaze and her thoughts back to the child. She could answer however she liked knowing that Sabrina wouldn't recall something told to her when she was already half asleep. Still, she wouldn't deny this child the comfort of the warm conversation she was asking for.

"Well, Sankeen partially means queen, a leader, and when necessary, a protector of those she is responsible for, to those whom she cares about."

The child's smile warmed Tendra's heart enough to produce a real smile, real warmth expressed in a tight hug and the pulling up of the covers past her shoulders.

Sabrina had more questions.

"What does the other part mean?" she mumbled between yawns. "I think it sounds like sweet queen."

"I like that," Sankeen agreed. She topped the moment off with a soft kiss to the child's forehead.

"Sleep well tonight, and tomorrow we can talk more about my name, okay?"

"Okay" fell from the child's lips as her eyes closed and she drifted off, adding the slight hint of an "hmm" sound as she slept. Sankeen replaced her smile with a flat lipped and expressionless demeanor, signaling that the time for warmth had ended. She turned toward Daniel, and they both stood.

"You have news?" she asked.

"Yeah, and it's not good," he replied.

Chapter Thirteen

DAY BROKE OVER the foggy grass hill as sunlight passed through the dense, hanging vines of several weeping willow trees. Kate sat shotgun in the SUV while Grimm Maro relaxed his wrists upon the steering wheel. Kate held Sabrina's doll, tinkering with it, trying to get it to work. What will it say? she desperately wanted to know.

Maro wanted to know as well. "Why are you toying with that thing? I haven't seen you put it down since you got into the car."

Kate was focused on the doll, very focused. "It's Sabrina's. I'm going to bring it to her when this is all over, something for her to hold onto once we get her back. She'll be scared, so this could help. It seemed to mean a lot to her before. I had one of these too when I was little. It used to say something, and I just can't remember what it was. It's killing me, I really can't remember, and I can't get it to work."

"You had *that* doll when you were a child? How old?"

Kate heard him but wasn't compelled to answer, still upset that he'd hijacked her mission.

"I remember one birthday, coming down the stairs

and seeing her on the kitchen table with a big bow in her hair."

"Pierce, how old were you?" he insisted.

"I don't remember, but it was such a great day," she recalled, feeling a sense of euphoric joy.

"Pierce," Grimm insisted, "how old were you? What birthday was it?"

Kate felt overwhelmed, and dizziness began to take over. "Whoa. I don't know, must have been six or seven, it's amazing how these things can bring back such strong memories and even stronger feelings."

"Pierce, are you sure you had that doll?" He had raised his voice; he commanded her attention.

"What do you mean?" She was starting to tear up. "I can't believe it's here, it's been so long, so long."

Grimm became visibly uneasy at Kate's growing instability.

Kate continued though, "I mean, what a coincidence that Sabrina had this doll, I mean, who would have thought? Such an old memory, you know?" Grimm pulled out and checked his gun, tightened his vest, and prepared for battle, rapidly. He turned and grabbed the doll and threw it out the window, fast.

"There's no such thing as coincidence, Pierce. You've been imprinted!"

"What? Why did you do that? What are you talking about?" But as soon as Kate said it, she knew what he meant and she saw it too. She acknowledged it before he could. "She planted the memory? Played with my mind, like you did at your house. Why? Why would an innocent child do that?"

Grimm realized it before Kate did. "I don't know. Maybe she's not innocent. Maybe she is, but she did it on purpose. They don't do that by accident."

"What do you mean? Do what? Wait, how do you know about that?"

"Never mind that now, we have to go. That feeling you're having, the euphoric dizziness, it means that she knows that you're here. She can feel you, and you can feel her."

"Why? How is that possible?" Kate wanted more answers, but Grimm was already out of the car. He popped the hatchback and put on his vest, handing Kate hers.

"Come on, Kate, you know why."

Kate didn't want to deny the feelings that she had for Sabrina anymore, but she never asked anyone who might know. "Is she my daughter?"

Grimm stopped, turned to her, and softened his voice. "You know she is, Kate. And she knows you're her mother."

He picked up the walkie and wielded his voice like a war drum, "GO! GO! GO!"

"Wait! How do you know that!" But it was too late, the tactical trucks and armored personal vehicles stormed down the road past them and he took off running after them. Kate would have to save her questions for later, but now she had another concern, another job on top of keeping Sabrina alive, she also had to make sure Grimm made it too or she might never get answers to her questions.

Chapter Fourteen

AGENT KATE PIERCE pulled her sidearm as the tactical team surrounded the farmhouse. The hidden faces masked by face gear resembled a hit squad if not for the letters, R.P.A. in giant, yellow letters strewn across their clothing, revealing that they were on the right side. Kate peered in through a window then radioed the team from a short distance.

"There are at least a dozen children inside. Be careful." Short words, she thought, long ones weren't necessary. It was time to go in and get her daughter back.

A hand waved a countdown: three, two, one. The front, back, and side doors were all kicked in simultaneously. Gunshots rang out immediately. Walkie chatter blasted through Kate's ear but she was focusing on running straight into and through the busted door and the ring of smoke surrounding it. Gun poised, she surveyed the room in an instant. Two down. *Theirs, not ours. Where's Sabrina? Where's Grimm?* she thought. In her mind, she was frantically running the scenarios of what the next room held. She turned, palms sweaty, gun ready.

"We have to go, we have to get out!" Daniel hollered at Tendra while she stood and watched the RPA agents flood the front lawn.

"I thought we had more time. Daniel, you said there'd be more time."

"I'm sorry, they're early, we have to go, we have to leave. We have to leave the children."

"What? No! I'm not leaving them!"

Daniel moved closer to Tendra. He turned her from the window and put both hands on her shoulders. She remembered every time he did that, like the first time, and she always replied by placing her hands on his face, which she did, but this time one of her hands had the weight of a pistol in it.

"Daniel, I love you, but I'm not leaving them."

"Even if it means you die? They don't want to take you in, Ten, they want to kill you!"

"I know."

"And?!"

"I won't leave them." She kissed him hard and turned away from him. She broke the four paned glass with the butt of her gun and fired three shots into the air.

"You're not getting them, so leave now! We won't miss this time!"

A barrage of gunshots rang out across the air, and Tendra and Daniel fell to the ground. From the floor she saw beams of light throughout the room; bullet holes in walls and door.

Daniel let out a groan.

"Daniel, are you alright?"

He sat up and looked around. He lifted his hand and there was blood.

"Oh, Daniel! No!"

"It's okay, it's okay, it's just a cut from the glass, look." He wiped away the blood and showed her a cut on his hand. "I'm okay, I'm okay."

"I'm so sorry, Daniel. I'm so sorry, I don't know what I was thinking; you're right, we have to go."

"Ten."

"What, what is it?"

"It's too late. They've surrounded us. We have to get into the attic, it's fortified, we can try to wait it out." Just as he spoke, gunfire rang out again, from outside the house and inside.

"They're engaging the agents. We have to get upstairs. We can keep the children safe from the gunfire if we get them up there too, but we have to go now!"

Tendra tried to think but she couldn't. She wanted to fight, but Daniel was right. She didn't care if she died but she couldn't let anything happen to Daniel, not like she let them kill Kellan. She knew it wasn't the same people, but it was the same risk. The humans would kill them all if they got the chance, and she couldn't let that happen.

"Let's go." She followed Daniel out the door into the bunk room with the kids. The children were huddled together in the back corner while Tendra's army fired back at the agents out the windows.

Tendra ran to Sabrina. "Sabrina, let's go, come with us! Get the other children!"

Sabrina stood and held her hand out to another scared, crying child. The child took Sabrina's hand and did the same to the next child, and the next. Tendra pulled on Sabrina's hand and they began to move, only to be stopped by a large explosion that shattered the walls. The children fell back, and only Sabrina was left holding onto Tendra. It took her a minute to realize she only had Sabrina when she looked back from running, but it was too late.

RPA agents filled the room, systematically shooting Tendra's soldiers. She ran, she only had Daniel and Sabrina, but if she could save them, then well, that was something, that was more than she could do for Kellan.

"The safe room! Now!" Daniel barked. Tendra leapt forward but lost the grip of Sabrina's hand. She turned. Sabrina had stopped and stood still.

"Sabrina, come on! Let's go now! They're coming!"

"I'm not going."

"Sabrina, stop it, let's go!" Tendra commanded. She was angry now. This was important, they had to go.

"I'm sorry. I know you want me to be safe and that's why I can't go."

"Tendra, Sabrina, let's go!" Daniel barked. "They're coming, we have to go!"

Tendra calmed herself and knelt down toward Sabrina while Daniel ran to the window to check on the agents' advancement.

"What's going on?" Tendra asked softly.

"The woman coming for me, Kate, is my mother, my real mother, and I need to wait for her."

"How could you know that? You don't know that."

"I do. So do you. We can feel it. We can feel each other, the ones we are connected to, genetically or not."

Tendra stared at the child. "When did you learn about genetics?" she asked.

"I didn't. I just know. I can't explain it, I just know it. I'm not like everyone else, I can feel it, Tendra. I was too scared to say anything before but now I can see what's going to happen if I don't do this. People will die, children will die, you will die. But if you go and I stay, that won't happen. I can see it clearly."

"I'm not leaving you here. They will take you and they will do things to you, Sabrina, horrible things."

"They will take me, yes, but the things you're talking about won't happen, not as long as she doesn't let them."

"Your mother? And how do you know—"

"She won't. I know."

"Oh no," Daniel jumped in. "Ten, they're coming through, it's too late."

Tendra kept her focus on the girl, on Sabrina. She smiled. Sabrina was right, they could feel it, they could feel each other and she felt it too; Sabrina would be okay.

"I love you."

"I love you too," Sabrina replied and jumped into Tendra's arms. "We're not done yet, don't worry, this isn't it."

Tendra nodded and turned away as Sabrina took a seat at the kitchen table. Tendra felt the stabbing pain of sadness take over, but with a deep breath she pressed on, out the door, and into the grassy field of wilted wheat crops behind the house.

Chapter Fifteen

AT A SMALL, retro kitchen table Sabrina was sitting quietly. Her daughter, there she was. She had that same doll that she'd left for Kate. Sabrina ran to Kate and hugged her. Overwhelmed, Kate knew that she needed to say something, but what?

"You're safe, you're safe now, I'm here," she assured her daughter.

"I was never in danger. But thank you for caring about me."

Kate looked around the room and saw an open door leading outside. Her expression gave her away.

"Sankeen is also *our* protector, like you. She is gone, but she'll be back soon."

"Okay, baby, let's get out of here."

Kate stood up, ready to take Sabrina out of the house, but to where she had no idea.

Grimm entered the room and locked eyes with the child.

"Grimm!" Sabrina ran to him.

"Hello, Sabrina. I am glad to see that you are safe. Were you scared?"

"No, I wasn't scared. I knew what to do."

Kate felt uneasy again, as if she was late to the party for a second time. First, who were the agents that were already inside? And second, what was going on here with Grimm?

"Sabrina, you know this man?"

"Kate, let me explain," Grimm tried to approach with a light hand, but Kate turned and stepped back from him, instinctually drawing her weapon back out of its holster.

"Stand back!" she said while pointing it at him.

"Kate, please, just wait a moment. I can explain."

But before he could, a gunshot echoed through the room with a deafening bang. Kate knew it wasn't her, she didn't shoot, but for a split second she questioned that fact only because of the multitude of mind tricks that had been played on her so far. But a fraction of a second later she saw the affect. It was Grimm, he'd been shot in the stomach and had collapsed. The assailant stood in the doorway, one of Tendra's soldiers. Kate trained her sight on him and took the shot. He was dead, but Grimm was on the ground.

Kate worked quickly to shut the heavy, wooden door and lock it from anyone else who might be looking for them. She sunk to the ground below the window and pulled Sabrina along with her. Blood formed from under Grimm's vest so Kate pulled it off and ripped his shirt open to find the wound, but jumped back when she saw his bare stomach and the telltale sign of a Traveler: three protruding belly buttons.

"What the hell?"

"Kate, let me explain."

"What's going on here? Sabrina, how do you know this man?"

"He was my doctor on the ship."

"He was? When you came to Earth?"

"No."

"What are you saying? Grimm, what is she saying?"

"He was on the ship when I was five. He was my doctor."

Kate was still confused, but she had an urge to ask a question of Sabrina, one that seemed simple enough to garner an answer.

"Sabrina, how old are you?"

"Fifteen."

Kate fell back again. "Aren't you nine? What is this, another trick?"

"Kate. It's not a trick. I left the ship years before it arrived. I had my orders. You should know this now, I never wanted to do these things, but I'm a soldier."

"What things?" Kate wanted to know.

"I'm trying to tell you something. Our children don't age like yours do. We haven't been here long enough for you to see, but some children, they age much more slowly."

"What are you saying? The children aren't really children?"

"I had my orders, Kate, I'm sorry. When I realized she was your daughter, it was too late, I couldn't–"

"Too late for what?"

Kate wanted more, she needed more, but she was interrupted by a horrible, terribly loud sound, like a fog horn mixed with a helicopter and a siren. It created a ringing in her ears, it blinded her and forced her to the ground. She could see two things: Grimm was dead. His eyes were open, and he was lifeless. Second, Sabrina was unaffected as she stood, walked past Kate with the doll in her hand, opened the door, and left. Kate forced her eyes open, crawled out the door, and was immediately in awe of the Traveler shuttle ship that was before her, in the middle of the wheat crop field. It encompassed all of the viewable space around her.

The shuttle door opened and Ringbak Arr and Dr. Lewis Marone stood at the craft's entrance.

Two men in Emigrati Guard uniforms emerged from behind the ship with Tendra and Daniel in cuffs.

Ringbak walked from the craft toward Tendra, and Marone toward Kate. Kate couldn't make out what was being said by Ringbak to Tendra but she saw one of the guards knock Daniel on the back of the head with a club. He dropped to the ground, and Tendra screamed before being carried onto the ship. Marone blocked the rest of her view.

"Hello, Agent Pierce, I'm Dr. Lewis Marone."

"I know who you are. What do you want? What is going on here?" Kate struggled to get the words out.

Kate elbowed herself up off the ground. She stood in front of Marone.

"She's a very special girl, isn't she?" he asked.

"Yes, my daughter is special."

Marone's chin tilted at the word "daughter."

"Yes I know who she is, and she is in federal protection now, and you need to leave here immediately," Kate declared.

Marone was unfazed by her threat. "Would you like to learn more about her?" he asked.

"What? What do you mean?"

He gestured with a head nod, and the men picked her up, not forcefully but with authority.

"Come, I will show you." Kate looked and saw another guard was carrying Sabrina onto the ship. She let out a brief, "Mom!" before disappearing inside.

"You have two choices, Kate. You can come with me about the shuttle and up to the ship where you'll be able to stay near your daughter, or you can stay here, wait for your superiors, and explain what the hell went so wrong here. It's your choice." He gestured to the ship.

Kate nodded, and the men put cuffs around her wrists.

"Just a precaution, you understand," Marone defended. "It will all make sense soon, I promise," he said with a duplicitous smile. Kate had no idea what was going to happen. She recognized the very real possibility that she could be killed as soon as she got to the ship, but what choice did she have? She had just been reunited with her daughter, and now she needed to get on that ship if there was any chance she could save her.

PART 3

Chapter One

The Year of the Arrival

DEEP WITHIN CENTRAL Africa, where warlords, dryness, and disease reigned, Dr. Lewis Marone emerged from a U.N. Medical tent. He was a tall, slender man with a grimacing disposition. He removed his level three, biohazard protective suit and went through the decontamination procedure. This procedure used to be foreign, reserved for dystopian tales of the future and zombie scenarios, but now it was much more widely recognized, especially in underdeveloped areas where a disease like Ebola spread without warning.

Following decontamination, Dr. Marone surveyed his surroundings, just another quick glance to ensure nothing had changed, just to make sure the seals of the tents remained intact. The villagers noticed him and of course all the U.N. medical gear, but they didn't seem phased by all the protective layers between them and the sick.

Marone had first noticed that this was sadly a normal existence for the people here. Medical tents, U.N. aide, foreigners with equally foreign equipment, invading their land and their space. This was now their standard way of life. He was just as used to it as they were, and that saddened him equally as much as the necessary interference he contributed to. His only joy came from the smile he permitted himself when he caught the small groups of village women sizing him up. They liked him, he was good-looking, after all, and he saved lives, but they teased him too, asking him when he was ready to contribute to the world, which in their eyes meant breed and procreate–with one of them.

He took his place at a small, wooden picnic table with built-in seats where his meal awaited. All eyes and ears were glued to a large television set, one that Marone felt was out of place in such a poor population. But that was technology and progress, he figured, easier and cheaper to get a fifty-inch television than it was to get medical care and education. He heard the news as the others did, about the alien ship that orbited Earth, about the year that had passed since it first showed up and communications that had ensued, and about the "Travelers," the aliens aboard the ship and their request to come down to Earth and integrate into society .

The villagers and other doctors fast-talked about the implications and the meanings, the genetics, the philosophy, but mainly the potential for disease. As the doctors spoke, one of them took the time to explain to the villagers that there was no way of knowing if the Travelers had any diseases, bacteria, or viruses that might be safe for them but deadly for people on Earth. For all anyone knew, the aliens could expel deadly toxins when they breathed. Most villagers seemed to grasp this idea, considering many of them had spent their lives making the choice between starvation or bush meat that could contain diseases like Ebola.

Dr. Lewis finished his meal calmly, peacefully, while watching as everyone else chattered. He moved slowly to clear his own plate even as the workers who surrounded him offered to take it from him. He knew that the villagers saw him as a god, he *was* one to them, descending upon their existence and wiping away their ills. It didn't hurt that he brought water purification equipment along as well. That was something they rarely saw, clean, clear water. Still, he cleaned his own plate, he didn't ask the locals to work for him. He finished washing it and he secured it in a sealed pantry of sorts so as to eliminate potential contamination from airborne elements. He always did these things in order to lead by example when it came to proper cleanliness and disinfection.

His personal tent was small and modest but with its own comforts, including a smaller but more current television which he never used. His pace suddenly quickened and he began to pack, ferociously.

His phone rang, but he didn't answer it. He knew by the 202 area code that it was from Washington D.C. The phone showed another voicemail had been left; it was the thirteenth voicemail sitting non-listened to. His satellite phone was next to ring, the one meant for vital communication back to the main research facility. Again, he ignored it; he knew it would only slow him down. With his bag over his shoulder, he moved to the back of the tent, to another zippered door, exiting where he couldn't be seen. If the villagers had any doubts that he was a god before, they'd be gone now as he had seemingly disappeared.

A woman peered into his tent and saw that he was gone, while at the same time a villager emerged from the medical tent, one who had been almost dead, one who Dr. Marone had healed and who was alive and healthy—a medical miracle.

Chapter Two

LOOKING OUT THE helicopter window, Dr. Marone stared down into the darkness of the deep Atlantic Ocean.

"Two minutes out, sir," popped briefly over static of the communications system and into his headphones.

"Thank you, captain," another man in fancy military clothes replied. He gestured toward the window next to Marone and pointed out into the distance. Marone raised his gaze to see an aircraft carrier sitting idle, surrounded by a variety of smaller Naval ships. They looked like gunships and were circling the aircraft carrier.

"Constant perimeter patrol," the military man explained. "When you've got that piece of equipment on board, you can't be too careful."

Marone could see what he was talking about now; next to the helipad was one of the Traveler shuttle craft. It looked like a wide body saucer but big–a transport of some sort, perhaps–and without wings or propellers. His first thought was whether it went up and down or forward and backward like a plane. It looked remarkably similar to the images of flying saucers from the 1950's but clean, very clean, like a brand new sports car. It was bright, shiny, and reflective, so reflective that when he squinted his eyes, it was as if it disappeared entirely.

The landing was quick and smooth, and through the noise and commotions, arms waved Marone toward a yellow, painted line that ran along the deck. He followed them and quickly came upon the saucer. It was massive, so much larger than it appeared from a distance. There was something else–the underside looked like skin. Not human skin, but almost rubber like a snake or lizard, but it was blended in to the hull of the ship. He liked this craft, he enjoyed the smile that it brought to his face, as he'd always dreamt of spaceships as a child. His childhood room had been adorned with replicas of almost every NASA spacecraft, including the ones that had gone to the moon.

When he was a young boy, his plans were to become a scientist and live aboard the space shuttle conducting experiments, but his call to service took him into human medical science instead, which wasn't important to the space science and experimentation program. He was excited to take the steps though, and he did, up the ramp and into the hull, which unfortunately looked very similar to any standard military transport plane cabin. Jump seats, tie downs, parachutes, it all looked just like the interior of some kind of Army plane.

Stepping aboard the alien craft, he was met by humans and not aliens. Four men were inside. As he crossed the threshold, he was keenly aware that he was now on an alien spacecraft, albeit an ugly one inside, and would, seemingly soon, be in space. Two pilots sat at controls in the forward cabin of the craft. A plainclothes man sat in one of the passenger jump seats and another military man who looked in charge sat beside him.

"Sir, I'm captain Reed, welcome aboard." A hand was extended but it was depressingly human; alien contact would have to wait. There were two military pilots at the controls who appeared to resemble a very new, clean, and updated military submarine control console. It looked very high tech but nothing about it looked alien. Captain Reed appeared as general issue as the seats, the floor, and the safety harnesses, except for his oversized and overexposed teeth. His smile almost masked his Vanderbilt or Davidson College accent; it was the kind of southern accent that screamed white glove, not redneck.

"Thank you, captain. Excuse me, but this all looks very..."

"Human?" Reed chuckled, but Marone didn't get the joke. Instead he disappointingly concluded that this was not an alien ship at all and was very much human.

"It is very alien, sir, I can assure you."

"But the controls, the seating ..."

"I don't pretend to know the motives of our friends up there, and it's above my pay-grade to consider, but I can tell you that from what we shuttle boat captains know, is that most of their tech feels human. It has something to do with not upsetting the order of things." Reed seemed unconvinced by his own explanation.

"Does everything look like this?" Marone wondered aloud.

"Not sure, sir, we just drive the boats."

"And they let you–us–fly them?"

Marone could tell by the look on Reed's face that he'd answered these questions many times already.

"It's a bit of a bumpy ride straight up so if you're ready, sir, we can strap in and head out. I'm sure whomever you're meeting with will have more answers than I do. Shall we?" Reed gestured to an available seat.

Lewis wasn't ready though. He was a doctor, a scientist, a man of data and discovery and he wanted more information before flying away in a strange, but neat, craft.

"Captain, I'd feel more comfortable if you could walk me through how this thing flies first, please."

The captain was ready to go, but instead of resisting, he relented and motioned to the pilots to shut down the ship and to walk to the rear of the craft.

"Pilot, this is Dr. Lewis Marone, special guest of POTUS. Could you please walk him through the operational mechanics of this craft before we depart?"

"Yes, sir," the pilot was quick to adhere to the command.

"Thank you, both," Marone countered.

"Sir, this vessel generates lift through a series of micro jet engines, each the size of about one large truck tire, kind of like a silent drone. Each engine works in sync with the rest to provide even lift. Each craft can hold enough fuel for one trip up, and once we push past gravitational pull it switches over to microwave thrusters or quantum vacuum plasma thrusters which moves us through space at a very high rate of speed."

"How long will it take?" Marone was uncomfortably uneducated on this subject.

"About five hours, sir."

"But that would put us at 50,000 miles per hour?"

"Yes, sir, the propulsion system allows for a self-generating, renewable energy in order to allow for a constant burn for the entire duration of the trip. We'll actually be traveling much faster than that at times but accounting for deceleration to the mother ship, it puts us right around an average of 50k miles per hour."

"Amazing."

"Dr. Marone, we've flown hundreds of man hours in these things and although they look pretty fancy, they don't really have any technology that we don't already have. The Travelers just packaged this candy up in a much nicer and more efficient wrapper." The captain was ready to go. "Shall we?"

Marone silently agreed with a nod and settled in for the trip, first making sure that his harness was secure. The odd looking, well dressed, government man who had been sitting and watching the whole thing unfazed or unimpressed offered an appreciative smile.

"Mason." He extended his hand, and Marone accepted with a firm shake.

"Lewis Marone."

"Yes, I know, I've heard a lot about your work throughout Africa."

"Sorry, have we met before? I don't recognize the name Mr. Mason."

"You can just call me Mason. No, we've never met, Dr. Marone, but the president and I spoke at great length about you."

"Sorry?"

"Dr. Marone, I'm the reason why you're here. Well, that's not really true, is it? The real reason that you're here is the advances that you've made in genetics. Particularly your work creating environments where introducing incompatible gene splicing actually works."

"Yes, well I assume that has something to do with why I'm here as well, but I thought we needed to test the alien environment for potentially dangerous toxins or contaminants?" Marone was a bit reluctant to enjoy this man's knowledge of his history, especially considering Mason's grin had turned from inviting to deceptive.

Mason was not done though, there was an encore to his little shuttle performance. "Of course, of course, but I can tell you that our preliminary data suggest that's all fine. You'll want to have a look at all that, I'm sure, but that's not the only reason that you're here, doctor." Mason turned to make eye contact. "It's that *other* work in Africa that will prove useful up there."

Marone knew immediately what he meant. Mason was talking about the time Marone spent with the CIA working on experimental genetic manipulation and administration. It was horrible. It was so very painful to the test subjects. He could still hear their screams and he had hoped that part of his life was over for good. But now it was front and center again, the dark shadow that pulled the light from his best accomplishments and humanitarian efforts.

The ship quickly took them up and out of the atmosphere. Marone felt the G-force as his ribs were pressed firmly into the back of his chest. The high-pitched wail of the engines seemed like it would never end and was growing more and more into a nails-on-chalkboard sound, and then suddenly it was gone, and the shuttle was as calm as could be. He was shocked at how smooth it was. He was finally doing it, his childhood dream of going into space was coming true. It made him smile, and Mason noticed, grinning back. "Enjoy it, doctor. It certainly is something special."

The ship sailed up and out of the atmosphere without incident. Marone knew they must be weightless even though he was fully strapped in and gripping hard to whatever he could. His shoelaces gave him away though; the loose one floated and fluttered above the rest. He let go, allowing his hands and arms to float. *Magnificent.*

"Okay, everyone, we're going to fire up the microwave and get this barbecue started. If all goes well, we should be docking with Traveler One in five hours." The captain's humor toward the potential for death was lost on Marone but not on Mason, who chuckled at the comments.

"This is my favorite part, Marone. Look out the porthole when we fire it up, it's a sight for sure." Mason was enjoying this, perhaps more so because Marone clearly was a space virgin. The captain flipped some switches, pulled some levers, and Marone saw a lighting sequence take place on the dashboard in the cockpit, followed by a low hum.

Marone looked straight ahead, not as interested in whatever Mason wanted him to see as much as he was in self-preservation, or at least the idea that he was somehow in control. He knew he didn't have any control at all and that thought provided a moment of calm, enough to look out the window, if you could call it that. It was more like a translucent skin that he could see through. Mason was right, it was magnificent.

A storm of colors flooded the area behind and

around the saucer. It was like a rainbow of unknown shades coming to life, grabbing onto the ship, and moving it forward before disappearing. It was something he never could have imagined and he was pretty sure he wouldn't ever be able to fully explain it accurately no matter how hard he may try.

"We've got some time to kill, doctor, do you mind if we chat?" Lewis could tell it wasn't really a question.

"Of course."

"Great. Doctor, these men have all been read in, and what I'm about to tell you, well, it's not something that a man in your field gets asked to do often, but with your intelligence and security clearance still intact, we thought you'd be the best man for the job."

"Go on." *Intriguing for sure,* Lewis thought, *What could this really be about then?*

"Let me be frank. We don't trust the Travelers, especially their leader, Ringbak Arr. All is a little too neat, tidy, and perfect with them, and to be blunt, those of us in intelligence don't like neat and tidy. It stinks. We've been accommodating and have been going along with them, and we fully intend to let them come down to Earth, but something isn't right and we need you to help us figure out what it is."

"Me? Why? What can I do?"

"Well, for starters, we want you to gain Ringbak's trust and befriend him, if possible. We think he's going to be excited to meet you, and our intelligence indicates that he needs someone with your particular skillset."

"My skillset? For what?"

"An invasion. No, I'm joking of course, well, not entirely. When the time is right, he is going to make a major announcement that will be a surprise to all of his kind and ours. All those aliens up on that ship share DNA with people here on Earth. They have relatives here."

"How is that possible?" His mind was flooded with questions, possibilities, and more questions, but he stayed quiet.

"We don't know. That's what we want you to find out. Ringbak claims not to know either, but we suspect he may. In fact, we think he's experimenting or examining his own kind in horrific ways. We need you to find out if there is some sort of hybrid experimentation program, and if so, gain his trust and be a part of it and report back to me about what you find out."

This was a defining moment, Marone thought. *Whatever I do now will forever alter my course in life.* This was the type of decision he would usually prefer to make with his wife, together, but it didn't look like he'd even get the chance to choose. It felt like the decision had already been made for him.

"I'll do whatever I can to help."

"Thank you, doctor. Your country appreciates your service."

Marone peered out the observation window, stretching his neck to watch the dance of colors taking place behind the propulsion system. The discomfort was more than he wanted to endure. He turned and looked ahead and saw their destination in the distance: the Traveler ship. *Time really does fly,* he thought, not realizing they had already made the distance.

Descriptions of its size didn't do it justice. It was massive, like the first time peering over the edge into the Grand Canyon, indescribably huge. He felt himself temporarily unprepared for the sensation that came with the amazement.

Reflecting the sunlight like an impossibly large S.O.S. mirror in the hands of a castaway, it shone bright, too bright. The captain indicated the need for the visor shield to be lowered and the pilot complied by pressing a few lighted buttons. A gold film encompassed the window.

"Get real sunburn off that thing if we don't lower the shade!" The captain was unusually pleased with this fact.

"It's not a real shade, of course. It's not like this thing has glass windows, but we don't have another name for it so, a shade it is," he remarked.

Even with the shield down, they could still see it, and as they approached, Marone's mouth grew wide, so wide that a hive of flies could gather inside his jaw if they wanted to.

"I never get bored of this part," Mason gleefully informed Marone.

"What about gravity?" Marone, always the scientist, wanted to know.

"They have that all worked out inside, another wonder of the mothership."

Mothership, that's exactly what it is, Marone thought. It was a bee hive, an ant Traveler, a constructed mobile civilization. The smooth, reflective, and round front end was in better view, but that tail, what was that tail? It jutted out like an antennae, so it could be that, but why would an advanced alien ship need what surely was an antiquated antennae? Those questions and more flooded his mind, but one stuck out, the same question that everyone wanted to ask but no one really did because there seemed to be no answer.

"Who built it?" That question was the new, "Are

we alone?" which had now been answered, of course. Marone wondered if it would ever be answered completely or if any answer would just lead to more questions. Academics had asked, of course. They were the most vocal voice when it came to questioning the mysteries of the Travelers, but no one had answered. Debates and hypothesis were all they had. Speculation really, nothing more.

The shuttle approached the underside of the Traveler vessel rapidly. It docked, ass end up, into the bottom of the ship. Marone grabbed the sides of his chair as the shuttle rattled and shook to the sounds of gears and pneumatics securing the shuttle into place. He took his cue from the rest, releasing his belt straps only after they had.

There was gravity. *How odd*, he thought, *How is that possible?* Pushing his feet against the floor, he stood up and, after a slight wobble, he was steady. A hatch door opened, but before he could leave the ship, the pilots and the captain began taking readings with what looked like Geiger counters, EMF detectors, and some other devices he didn't recognize.

"Just a moment, doctor," the captain said. "Just need to make sure we're all good here. Yup, looks fine. You boys enjoy your visit. We'll be here waiting when you're done."

Marone looked into the bright white hallway beyond the hatch. It could have been that looking onto the darkness of space for the last few hours just made the hallways appear that way, he realized, but it really was very bright.

The silhouette of a single individual appeared in the doorway.

"Doctor Marone, I've been eagerly awaiting your arrival," the voice said. He recognized that voice as Ringbak Arr. He was taller than he appeared on television, very tall, but incredibly disarming with a warmth and smile of sincerity. His was alone.

Ringbak approached and extended his hand to Marone. Mason intervened, "Doctor, I'm sure you can understand that we're not one hundred percent sure that it's safe to have skin to, well ... skin contact."

"What percentage says that it is safe?" Marone fired back.

"Excuse me?" a confused Mason responded.

"You said you're not one hundred percent sure, so how sure are you that it is safe?" he interrogated Mason with this question, but knew this would be vital to the psychology of building trust with the alien leader.

"Sir, we are under strict protocol to run our tests prior to making physical contact with the Travelers," the other military man answered, but Marone didn't turn, holding his posture toward Ringbak's hand and his eyes toward Mason.

"Seventy-nine percent that it's safe," Mason finally revealed.

With that, Marone grasped the alien's hand, and shook and held and smiled, and most importantly, started a bond that he hoped would be vitally important in the future.

"The pleasure is all mine, sir, the pleasure is all mine." Marone meant it too.

Distant stars swung by in the night sky, no longer illuminating her life. Tendra watched Earth disappear behind her, and the reality of where she was going began to set in. She hadn't been on that ship since they left–her and Kellan. So much had changed since then. So much was different, in her especially.

She glanced past the seated heads at the front of the ship and out into space. She raised her cuffed hands to push the hair from her face and, one at a time, tuck some behind her ears.

She had been so excited to go down to Earth. There'd been so much possibility ahead for them. They were supposed to go to New York, see Broadway shows, travel to the mountains, and swim in the ocean. She wanted to buy dresses, hundreds of them, and model every one of them for Kellan, hoping that he would remove them one by one before they made love. She remembered the surprises she had planned for her Kellan once they arrived. She was going to take him to the shore where a sailboat would be waiting with an instructor for them. Kellan would have loved to sail, she knew it; he would learn all about how to do it, and then she was going to surprise him by renting one for them to use for a whole month.

She knew he would want to explore the planet. She had studied all about Alaska, California, and Paris. Oh Paris, she had very special dresses prepared for that trip. That's where the romance would take over them both, and she was sure her love would have proposed to her. She expected they would explore every inch of that green planet and then find their place, their home, and have kids of their own, raising them like other Earth children.

None of that happened. It brought a single tear to her eye, which dropped, sizzling when it hit the tactical pants that she wore now, a stark reminder of who she had become, a blatant clue as to what this world had made her into. She was a killer. She was cold, and while she tried to love Daniel, she admitted to herself that it was just companionship. Kellan was her only true love, she realized that now. Would they have done all that they set out to do, or would he still have been killed by a raging mob of extremists? Maybe humans just genuinely sucked, horrible in every right. All the what ifs consumed her. What if they hadn't been separated, what if the humans didn't hate Travelers, what if she hadn't gone to meet him on Broadway? He'd still be alive. What if she agreed never to leave the ship like he first wanted? All of it hurt, but none of it mattered. She knew what had to be done. Kill Ringbak, Marone, Kate, and everyone on that ship, and then destroy it. She wanted to destroy everything she could before she died, which she planned would also happen on that ship.

But how? she wondered quietly. This helped her rage, to think out a plan. Ringbak had some powers, she thought. She looked over at him as he talked with Marone. She really wanted them both dead, but she shook her head to help her refocus. Ringbak and Marone both turned and looked at her. Never the mind–how, was the question. How did he do what he did back on the ground? How did she do some of the things that she did herself? Killing the men who killed Kellan was effortless. She looked down at her hands and the burn on her pants from the tear. Heat! That had to be the answer. She felt hot when she killed. She felt hot when she was angry. Her tears could burn. She looked at her hands.

Were they the answer all along? she wondered, anxiously interrogating her own mind. She looked up to make sure no one was watching, and when she was sure, she tucked her hands down into her crotch and pressed her eyelids tight, clenched every muscle in her body and tried to burn the handcuffs. Nothing happened, which was probably a good thing since the guard sitting next to her was monitoring her closely. Then she saw it. A single drop of sweat rolled off his forehead. It could have been a coincidence; it could just be hot in there. But then she saw another sweat bead, then another. Soon he was sweating profusely, shifting his position in his seat.

"Guard, what's the matter?" Ringbak shouted back from his position.

"Sorry, sir, I'm just, it's just, I'm getting really hot." As if those words were important to Ringbak and Marone, who looked at each other for a moment before they turned back and saw what Tendra had somehow done: everyone in the shuttle was sweating. Everyone except Tendra and Ringbak. He noticed that fact as well. He stared at Tendra, and she felt him, deeply. It was an intimacy that she hadn't felt in a long time, but instead of love it felt to her like a moment of high tension with someone she loved, it felt like the moment before a fight. Then it was gone and so was the heat. The temperature seemed to retreat back to normal. Still, she had no idea how she'd made it happen, what she'd made happen.

Just to be safe, she tucked her cuffed hands deeper into her lap. She went back to her thoughts of death and killing them all, but this time she had a weapon, even if she didn't know how to use it yet. She wouldn't have any more time to figure it out either. The ship was in front of them now. As it grew closer, she thought again of the last time she was here, she recalled holding Kellan's hand tightly in her own. Now, she was only holding her own hand, that and cold, metal cuffs.

Kate worked through the plans in her head. If she could get the cuffs off, grab Sabrina, and escape, how would they get off the ship? How would she get the cuffs off, how could they get away from Ringbak, Marone, and his guards?

She looked down. Sabrina sat next to her. At least they let her have that. She smiled down at Sabrina, and Sabrina smiled up, nestling herself into the crook of Kate's arm. Kate had gone through so much, all this time, all she'd gone through with the doctors, the bouts of abdominal pain, the attacks, and then reuniting with this girl, her daughter. She had a daughter; she couldn't hardly believe it. It had all happened so fast she never got a chance to open her arms or to ask the obvious questions. How did this happen? Who were the Sutcliffes then if Kate was her real mother? And even more puzzling, who was the father? So many thoughts, so many questions, and so much she wanted to do when this was over, to do with Sabrina, her daughter. How would she raise her as a single, working mother? Would she even have this job if she made it out alive? Oh god, making it out alive, that was a real, very real concern, and the fear became present. The sour feeling in her stomach, the nausea she felt, wasn't a bout but a new thing, the feeling she got when she thought about making it out alive with Sabrina. She needed a plan.

Kate looked across the seats at Tendra. She was flush, getting more and more red in the face. She

looked like she was about to explode with rage. Kate
didn't want her to get in the way when it was time to
escape, so she needed to diffuse her, or at least try.

"Tendra, you're lucky that you're not still on Earth.
Wherever they are taking you will be better than what
would have happened to you if you stayed, I can assure
you of that."

"Sankeen. My name is Sankeen. Tendra died on the
streets of New York when your people killed Kellan."
Kate didn't have a response. She wanted Tendra
punished, but she did feel bad for her. How could she
not? She'd lost everything.

Sankeen continued, "I am saving these children,
my children. I tried to tell you, I asked you to look into
it on your own, but did you?"

Kate did not, but couldn't admit it.

"Of course you didn't, why would you? You think
you're helping these children? I can promise you that
you are not."

"Look, you may not like it, but we are the best
chance that these kids have at normalcy. No system is
perfect, but it's you and the other terrorists who are
causing these kids hurt, not us," Kate defended.

"Ha! I'm hurting them? Me, Travelers? What a joke
you are, all of you." Tendra looked away from Kate.
She stared straight ahead, and Kate could hear the
damage in her voice, "Do you have any idea, now that
you're here, in cuffs like me, that something more is
going on? Can't you see it at all, any of it?"

Of course Kate could tell this wasn't right. She was
a federal agent in cuffs, this was definitely not okay.

Tendra continued, "The Travelers that you think
are being sent to live with families aren't staying with

them for long. They are dropped off by you, and just as fast as they arrived, they are taken, drugged, and experimented on. Your government, you humans, you're the ones torturing these kids, and you're just as guilty as those two." Tendra stared stiffly at Ringbak Arr and Dr. Lewis Marone.

The shuttle approached the Traveler ship. Kate had never seen it this close before, not even on TV or online. It really was massive, and shiny, so shiny. Being underneath it felt like being underwater, staring up at the surface, the brightest thing in her view. In a few minutes the hatch doors would open and Kate still didn't have a plan. She felt suddenly powerless. Her surroundings were so foreign, how could anyone know what to do in this situation? There were too many guards, too many men, too many handcuffs. Without the cuffs off, this would be much harder than she had hoped. For now, as much as it bothered her to realize it, she had to go along until an opportunity presented itself.

The shuttle bumped with the mothership. Metal on metal clinked and clanked the passengers to life, shaking them as the shuttle settled into place. A swishing sound like a pneumatic press proceeded the hatch door opening. Everyone stood, everyone except Kate, Tendra, and Sabrina.

Ringbak gestured toward the back, and the guard sitting nearest Tendra took her by the cuffs and stood. but Ringbak wanted more. "Bring the child also."

"No!" Kate jumped to her feet only to be met with a staff to the gut, which dropped her back down to her seat. She struggled to catch her breath and call out for her daughter as they pulled her away, "Sabrina!"

"Mom!" For once, this child didn't want to go with anyone. She reached out for Kate, and Kate reached back for her, but just as their hands touched, she was ripped away, carried off by the guard with Ringbak and Tendra.

She was gone. Again.

Kate's heart sank. Watching Sabrina walk away made her ill. She leaned over and threw up. Then she cried.

"You can leave us," Marone ordered the last remaining guard.

"But sir, I have orders to ..."

"And leave me the keys to her cuffs."

"But, I, well ..."

"Son, this woman is a federal agent in the United States Department of Homeland Security. Do you think it wise to stick around while she is kidnapped by aliens? Leave the keys and go, and you won't have to lie when you're interrogated about what took place here."

The guard looked at Kate and Marone, then back at Kate. She saw his expression change. She knew he was giving in, and with a shrug of his post-teenage shoulders, he tossed the keys to the floor in front of Marone and fled the scene. Now it was just the two of them, and her cuffs were coming off. *One roadblock down*, she thought.

Kate rubbed her wrists and felt the freedom of their movement. "What did you do that for?" she asked. He looked out into the corridor and turned quickly toward her with a hurried expression. He grabbed her by the arm, powerfully but not aggressively.

"Listen, there's not a lot of time," was all he could

get out before Kate punched him in the throat. She jumped up, grabbed his arm, twisted it, and in one quick move she had him down, his body in between her legs and his throat between her arms. He gasped for breath.

"Wait, wait! Kate, please let me explain!" he managed to squeak out.

"Why should I? You kidnapped a federal agent. I can shoot to kill just based on that alone, and if what they said was true and you are a monster who tortures innocent children, then why shouldn't I end you right here and now?" She allowed herself to be lost in her anger. Her fear for what might happen to Sabrina was the only necessary motivator.

"That girl is your daughter," he let out in a raspy, choked voice.

"Of course she is, I already know that." She pressed in harder on his throat while grabbing the handgun from inside his waistband.

"She's different though. She's ... not what you ... think."

"You think I can't see that? I don't know what you did to her, but when I find out I'm taking this whole thing down, starting with you right here." She moved her arms around to tighten her grip on his neck.

"I can help you both escape. You neeeeeed me." She wanted to let go, but Kate knew that part was true. She had never been on this ship before and had no idea how to find Sabrina and escape. But it was his final, struggled words that mattered most. The cuffs were off, that was important, but she still had no idea what to do next or where to go. She let him up, but stood and pointed the gun right at his head.

Marone struggled to catch his breath, hunched over on all fours, vulnerable.

"If this is some kind of trick, I swear I'll kill you," Kate warned.

"That, Agent Pierce, I have no doubt about. Your honesty and integrity are the reasons why we chose you for this job, why I wanted you."

"What are you talking about?" Another trick? She didn't trust him and doubted whatever he was about to say was the truth and there wasn't anything that would get her to lower the gun, but he went on.

"I am also a federal agent. I work for the CIA. My mission was to find out why Ambassador Arr was kidnapping Traveler children and what he is really up to, and if possible, stop it."

"Why should I believe you?" she wanted to know. What could he tell her to prove his claim?

Marone pushed himself up off the ground and stood before her, shaking his head with a tiredness. His slow breath of words informed her, "What choice do you really have?"

He was right.

She cocked the pistol. "How do we get my daughter back and get off this ship?" she demanded.

"We start by you trusting me," he pleaded.

"Then you better tell me everything and hope that I believe you by the time we find her or else I'm pulling this trigger once we do."

"I understand. Let's hurry, this way. There's a part of the ship that few know about, that's where they'll take her." She knew he understood her, but still, she needed to keep the gun on him, just in case.

"After you."

Tendra followed behind Ringbak, with Sabrina at her side. She could protect the child as long as possible, and if she couldn't protect her then she could at least be there for her, be next to her like she did in the nursery, for all of the children that she cared for.

She scanned the room but never took her hands off Sabrina. She wondered if someone would see them. If they did, then she could make a noise, draw their attention, and that would be her chance for them both to escape.

Ringbak stopped in the middle of the corridor. He looked back toward Tendra and scanned the halls. He placed his palm on the wall, the empty, shiny, white wall, and it glowed a dull red. A hidden door opened before them, and he gestured for the guard to push her and the child through.

Once inside, Ringbak joined them, and the door shut behind them. Lights turned on, illuminating another hallway indistinguishable from the others, except this one was eerily quiet and totally empty.

Tendra knew that she had to make a move. She should have before they entered the room but now she had no choice; she needed to get Sabrina out of there. After everything going on, she still wanted to keep her safe. But there weren't any options. The hallway went on forever and she could see no way out. She feared what might be at the end of the corridor. The only option was back.

They walked for three more minutes, then they exited into another hallway, but this one wasn't hidden. She recognized where they were by the large, vault-like doors in front of them. They were at the entrance to the propulsion room, the one place that no one had ever been able to enter, not even Ringbak. The corridor must have just been a way to keep Ringbak and whomever hidden while they were moving through the ship full of Travelers. But why use it now? There couldn't be more than a few dozen left on the ship. These days there were more VIP tourists than actual Travelers.

Once again, Ringbak placed his hand on the wall and the doors, and the ones that never opened and supposedly no one had ever seen, slowly began to open.

"You can access this room?" Tendra questioned Ringbak. Every Traveler was taught that this room was sealed off by their ancestors, by whoever sent them away on the ship, and none of them were able to access it, even though Travelers and humans both tried.

"Yes. I am allowed in. Today, you will be allowed in as well. You're about to learn more than any other Traveler ever knew about this ship." The guard took a slight step back, the confused look on his face confirmed to Tendra that he was not a part of Ringbak's plan, or team, for that matter. Maybe she could turn him. Once they got inside, she could convince him to help her, to take off her cuffs so that she could kill Ringbak.

Her thoughts were murdered by the deafening sound of a gunshot ringing through the hollow corridor. The guard dropped to the floor, and Ringbak held the gun.

The doors opened. She knew it was now or never. She rushed Ringbak and, with her cuffed hands, thrust the gun up into the air, forcing him to stumble.

"Run! Run, Sabrina, run!" And she did. Sabrina turned and bolted down the hallway and around a corner before Ringbak could gather himself.

"You don't know what you're doing, Tendra," he said as he regained his footing, picked up the gun, and tucked it away into his belt. "You think you're helping her but you're not," he screamed at her. He never screamed or yelled. Not once had anyone ever witnessed him raise his voice.

"She has a very important role to fill in our survival, all of us, and you're just delaying that. You can't stop it!"

"Maybe not, but I can still try."

Ringbak grabbed her by the cuffs and tossed her into the room. He grabbed the guard's dead foot and dragged his body in before the doors shut them both in.

The room was dark. It looked shallow like a large, empty storage compartment. Ringbak used the pistol to wave Tendra further inside.

"She will be brought back to me, you're wasting your time. I think when you see what's in here you'll stop this foolishness and come to see that this is all for our kind, to survive here amongst all those who want to see us dead."

"How can you justify what you are doing to these children? Torturing them, scarring them. I know what you're doing, I've seen the evidence, all the documents."

"You've got it all wrong. We're not hurting them; we're giving them life."

In unison, dozens, hundreds of lights click on and sprang to life. The room was deep, that wasn't even the right word for it. It wasn't a room at all, it was an entire part of the ship, it was deeper than she could see. After the overhead lights came on, one by one, smaller, purple lights flicked to life throughout the cavernous space, illuminating tubes that looked like giant lava lamps.

Tendra squinted her eyes to get a better look, and as her eyes adjusted, she could see they weren't purple lights, they were tubes of purple liquids, floor to ceiling, and the lighting behind them made them appear as though they were lights in and of themselves. She saw something floating in one of them, in all of them, and walked over to the closest one to inspect it.

Then the horror, the madness of what she was looking at became clear. It was a child, but not just any child. It was Max, one of the Traveler children she'd cared for. She darted to the next one, it was Clara, the next one Quinta, then the next one. The next one made her drop to the floor. She pressed her hand up against the tube and cried as she saw the lifeless body of another child.

"Ben. What have they done to you?" Hope dropped from her body, and civility fled from her mind. She felt something new, something that she never wanted to feel–defeat. A thousand punches to the stomach by the person you loved the most. It was as if Kellan, her true love, was the one kicking her while she was down.

The tubes were all filled, not just with children, but all ages of Travelers, hundreds, thousands maybe, one in each of the tubes. They all had three tubes running to their tipple belly buttons, and all had their eyes closed.

"What is this?" she demanded of Ringbak.

"This is survival, this is eternal life. This is our future. When the children arrive on Earth, they change. They emit a signal, that's the best way to describe it. They could interact with the area around them telekinetically in a way. The become smarter, sharper, and powerful. Most have no idea, but they will once they're older. To put it simply, they have gifts. But these gifts didn't get birthed into existence until they were on the planet for a few months. So once they were down there long enough ..."

"You brought them back up, and what, cloned them?"

"That's a simplistic way of looking at them. These are not clones, these are real, flesh and blood sentient beings. They will be capable of incredible things once they're ready."

She pulled herself up, contemplated how she would end everything, and wandered between the tubes, taking in the stabbing pain she felt with each Traveler face. Her heart raced, her breath quickened, and her skin boiled. She felt rage again, she felt every muscle tighten and both eyelids widen fully.

One tube behind them came alive with light and the swirling purple goo. She saw a figure moving around inside but couldn't see its face.

"Hello, Tendra," a female voice called out from nowhere. Tendra looked around quickly but couldn't see who was talking. Ringbak stood silent, watching her, and lowered the gun he had pointed on her.

"Or should I call you Sankeen, the Bloody? You've certainly made a mess of things, haven't you?" the voice demanded her attention.

"Who's there? Who are you? How do you know me?!"

A panel lit up a large control system with an even larger screen above it. The space around them "turned on" and there was a moving image of the Milky Way

Galaxy swirling around and in between them.

"Where is the child?" the voice asked. "We need to put her through."

"She'll be here soon," Ringbak answered.

A moment of silence played out as Tendra studied the images before her. A point appeared, indicating the solar system and Earth within it. A line emerged from Earth and spread across the galaxy to another point, another system and an Earth-like planet. From there, another line emerged, then another, and then one more. Five points between the Milky Way and lines to three other galaxies were connected.

"What is this?" Tendra demanded of them both.

"Tendra, there is much more going on here. Your stupid, little war is making things difficult for us."

"Difficult for who? You? The humans?" She could feel the tightness again. Her muscles constricted.

Ringbak put his hand on her shoulder. "This is Mother, for lack of a better term. She is, and has been, our guide throughout this journey."

Mother took over, "I am an artificial intelligence designed to connect and reprogram eight different species from different parts of the universe. You, along with the others, represent thousands of years of breeding and genetic manipulation in order to ensure that all of you survive the ever-changing dynamics of your environments. My job is to make sure that happens, to make sure you survive."

Tendra needed more answers. "I don't understand. How long has this been going on? We were only on the ship for one generation."

"You've been on this ship for nine hundred years. Every one hundred years I reset and rebirth you all and update your DNA and the technology aboard the ship. There are five other ships like this one and we communicate with each other and share genetic data and samples back and forth to help with each reset."

"So you know where we came from?"

"You didn't come from anywhere. You came from here. You were evolved aboard this ship as it circled this system. I was able to send craft down to Earth as needed to get the information and DNA for the procedures until you and the rest were ready."

Tendra couldn't believe her own ears. She tried to muffle Mother's voice, but her cuffed hands wouldn't allow it.

Ringbak moved closer to her. "You have to see now, this isn't what we wanted, this fighting. We are the good guys here, we are the ones who want to survive and live, and now it is our time, it is our turn on this planet. We are the new human, the new Earth people, it is our place to refresh this entire system."

"Wait, what are you talking about, our time?"

Mother interjected, "A final reset is needed. We are going to cleanse Earth of the current humans once we have enough of you in order to ensure the survival of the Travelers. Their time has ended, and I need to ensure a clean genetic line is established. And we need to correct your path and realign your actions as such."

A low rumble emerged, followed by pneumatic sounds and pressure releasing from the tubes Tendra was observing. Two of the chambers drained, spilling the purple goo all over the floor. From the steamy haze of the purple tube, the first figure emerged. She could only see the feet at first, they were bare, but a man's set. Then she saw him and her heart stopped, for a moment at least. Kellan stood before her, naked and alive.

Ringbak spoke again, "When you forced Kellan to leave the ship and go into hiding it upset a very delicate plan that was to ensure your survival as a species. Now, we need to restart that plan."

With those words, Kellan woke up–coming to life, it seemed. "Tendra!" he yelled, running to her, wrapping his slippery arms around her.

She pulled her cuffed hands up to his face as if feeling it would prove he was real, that this was all real.

"Kel, what happened, is this real, are you alive?" She couldn't hold back. As much as she wanted to kill everyone around her, here standing before her was the one Traveler that she was doing it all for. But now he was alive.

"I don't know, yes, I mean I am real, but the last thing I remember is being taken from you at the immigration check point. What are we doing back here?"

"Oh, Kellan."

He looked like a child to her, like one that she cared for, like Benjamin who floated in a nearby tube. She softened, "We went down but we were separated and they took you, and I couldn't find you. I didn't see you for a long, long time. When you showed back up you were murdered right in front of me."

He pulled away from her. "What?" His confusion was real, she could tell.

Ringbak pulled his son back toward him and for a moment he was blind to Tendra. She clenched every muscle in her body, held her breath, and pushed air through her own eyeballs. She tried to force so much pain on herself to bring back her power, to use that heat that helped her before, even if she had no idea how to do it. It worked. Her handcuffs melted off, and with bloodshot eyes she dropped to the ground, rolled into a somersault, pulled one single bear claw knife from her boot, and stood up to Ringbak's neck. She held it to his throat and took position behind him, ready to slice him dead.

"You did this to him! No matter how you justify it, you did those same experiments on him to get to this, didn't you? I didn't know what I was reading before but it makes sense now, you have to torture them to do this, to enhance them and clone them, don't you? Why don't you tell him how you had him kidnapped and taken to Alaska to be tested on?"

Kellan, still looking confused, asked for confirmation from his father, "What is she talking about? Why don't I remember anything?" he yelled, making his own anger apparent.

Ringbak was calm; he didn't flinch. Tendra wondered why he wasn't concerned.

"Yes, I did all of that, son, and I'm glad that I did," he answered.

"See! I told you, Kel, he's trying to hurt you!" Tendra felt momentarily vindicated.

"It's true that I had you taken, but not to hurt you, but to save you. And I'm glad that I did."

Kellan echoed what they were both thinking, "What do you mean, help me?"

The other tube, the one next to Kellan's opened up. The sounds of gushing liquid were enough to get everyone's attention. Another silhouette emerged and stood by Kellan. It was Tendra, a new, fresh, version of her. This one was almost lifeless, empty like a shell, still, vacant behind its cold eyes, silent.

Tendra was losing control, she could feel it. "What the hell is this? Who is that? Whose is that?" she demanded of Ringbak.

"Kellan didn't want to go down to Earth, did he? He wanted to stay at first and be safe, he wanted to keep you safe. You were the one who insisted, pressured him, forced him to do what you wanted."

"I ... I ... we, we were just ..."

"If you had stayed on the ship then none of this would have happened. I took him, yes. I did it so that we could get his sample, the one that he was supposed to give the night you left. I wanted to ensure that if anything happened to him that he could be reborn, and I'm glad I did because you got him killed."

"Ten, what's he talking about?" Kellan clearly didn't remember.

"No, that's not what happened!"

"Isn't it? You went to New York and he came for you, and was killed because of you. You killed him and you gave me no choice!" Ringbak shouted.

Kellan struggled with his words, "Tendra, I ... I..." He couldn't speak normally and looked like he was getting sick, falling to his knees.

"You're killing him, Tendra, again. His body may look ready, but his mind is not. His memories are at odds with what you are doing here."

"Then fix him! Put him back in, fix him!" Tendra demanded.

Mother took over, "We can do that, Tendra. I can do that, but for it to work you both need to be reset."

Tendra knew, somehow, exactly what Mother meant. She allowed herself the thought of a reset, of starting over, putting it all back together and having a life with Kellan, the life she wanted now more than ever, even if this version of her would have no memory of any of this.

Kate walked down the long, desolate hallway with her gun behind Marone's head.

"Where is everybody?" she asked.

"It's mostly just tourists these days, not many Travelers left up here."

Kate heard voices from another end of the hall and pushed Marone up against the wall. There was nowhere to hide. There was nothing but long halls with no doors.

Marone went for his breast pocket, and she pressed her gun into his neck.

"Whoa, just getting my badge." Marone pulled his badge out slowly.

Marone pulled out a silver, metallic card with a chip in the center. He pressed it against the wall, and a hidden door opened. Kate heard the voices getting closer and pushed Marone in, following after him. The door shut behind them but became transparent as a tour group moved past.

"Can they see us?"

"No. It's like a two-way mirror."

Kate looked around another long, empty hallway, only it was much narrower.

"What is this?"

"Just a shortcut."

"Then why do you need that?" She pointed her gun at the badge in his hand.

"You know, we can move a lot faster if you put the gun down."

Kate considered it for a moment. She didn't want to lose Sabrina over the need to keep Marone in her sights.

"Fine, but if you even flinch in the wrong direction, I'm pulling the trigger."

"You see those doors at the end of the hall? The ones with the markings on them? That's where we need to get to."

"What is it?"

"It's everything, Kate. It's the truth."

"And what's that exactly? The truth?"

"They're not here to live amongst us, Kate. They're here to replace us, but they don't even know it. Well, no one except—"

"Ambassador Arr," Kate filled in.

"Yes. I don't even know if he really knows what's going on."

Kate motioned for him to keep moving, "Go on."

"The ship is alive, sort of. It's run by an A.I. that has been directing the ambassador's every move since the beginning. You see, this is a god ship, Kate. It didn't come from anywhere, it's always been here and its purpose is to continually evolve the human race. But in order for the evolution to work, she—"

"She?"

"Sorry, I've gotten used to looking at her like a mothership. It has to make sure the current population doesn't mix with the new population while it assembles enough new humans to populate the planet."

"And how does it plan to do that?"

"That's the problem, we don't know. I've been trying to find out exactly how it's going to remove us but I can't figure it out."

"So what's that have to do with me?"

"Sorry, Kate, I misled you back there. You weren't chosen for this but I needed you and you need me."

"Need me for what?"

"We need to kill Ambassador Arr and destroy the A.I."

Kate wanted to respond, but something caught her attention. "Sabrina!" she shouted as Sabrina ran past a translucent window in the hall. Kate grabbed Marone's badge out of his hand and pressed it to the wall. It opened a door just big enough for Kate to grab Sabrina and pull her inside.

"Are you okay? What happened? Did they do anything to you?"

"I'm okay, Mom."

Those words made Kate cry. The love she felt for this child wasn't some trick of the mind or emotions, it was real and she could feel it's realness.

"I'm so sorry, I'm so sorry, I have you now, I've got you," she said as she pulled Sabrina to her. "How did you get away?"

"Tendra. She helped me."

"Sorry, Kate, we need to go now, while we have the chance," Marone interrupted their moment.

"Go? Why? I have her back. Get us out of here, get us back down to Earth like you promised."

"We can't leave now. Didn't you hear what I said? They're going to wipe us out!"

"Why do you need me? Why can't you do it?"

"I don't need you."

Suddenly it dawned on Kate. "He won't stop coming for her, will he?"

"No."

"Why? What do they want with her?"

"She's evolving, Kate. She's the next step, the one that they need to pull from, to mix with the others. She's got gifts that the rest of us can't even imagine. She knew it was true. Just like she was able to manipulate others, Sabrina had something special going on inside of her."

Ringbak was trying to use her for something, Marone was trying to use her for something, even Tendra or Sankeen, whatever she was calling herself, wanted Sabrina. But this was her child, her daughter. She was not giving her up, she didn't have to.

Sabrina spoke, "It's okay. I need to go in there. I am necessary," she said stoically.

"For what? I just got you back, I'm not letting you go in there."

"He's right, what he's trying to explain. The plan to kill you all, all of humanity, and I can stop it."

"Why you? You're just a child!"

"You know why. I can do things that other Travelers can't. There's something controlling this ship, I can feel it, maybe I can stop it. That's what you want, isn't it?" She looked at Marone, then Kate.

Kate looked into her daughter's eyes and wept. She didn't want to believe it. She didn't want to allow it. She looked up at Marone. His eyes told the same story. This was the only way.

Kate managed the words the best she could, "Okay."

Kate, Marone, and Sabrina approached the solid blast doors to the propulsion room. Kate put her hand up to the alien metal and felt the indentations and the burn marks that surrounded them. Marone pulled his badge and pressed it to the door, but it didn't work. Sabrina stepped forward and moved his hand away.

She looked toward the door while Kate scanned the area, pistol held tightly in her hands. "Sabrina, what are you doing?" she whispered.

Sabrina raised her hand to the door and moved it around, pressing herself closer as if trying to feel for something. Then she stopped, and a red light appeared behind her palm. The doors slowly opened up.

Kate thrust herself into the room first. "Everybody freeze! Hands in the air!" she demanded. She could see Tendra had a knife to Ringbak's throat and two other Travelers were standing there as well; both were naked and dripping. She could see the tubes behind them, she could see the purple goo on the floor. She could remember her nightmares. It was starting to make sense to her now. The feeling of floating, the purple was so clear, the goo, the umbilical cord, she'd been in these tubes as well, swimming in the purple mess and watching while her stomach grew to the size of a basketball.

She set her gun on Ringbak, but he was already under Tendra's knife. She adjusted it to Tendra's head.

"What is this place?" she asked.

Tendra responded, "Why don't you ask him?" She glared to Marone. "He and the rest of them have been kidnapping, torturing, and cloning our children, the Traveler children."

"It's not that simple, Tendra," Kate responded. "He's not who you think."

"Huh. Human. You're just as bad as the rest of them."

Kate aimed her gun at Ringbak, or Tendra, she

couldn't decide. She didn't know what to do. She just knew they both needed to be taken down.

Ringbak suddenly stepped forward and turned from Tendra. She tried to lunge at him but was frozen. She couldn't move no matter how hard she tried. Ringbak held his hand out low, in control of her, she could feel it, as if there was a cable line tethered between them. He moved away from her easily.

"It's time for a reset. It's time to start this over with you two, and get it right." The other Tendra moved to Kellan's side and held his hand. "You are all thinking so simply. You still cannot comprehend what you are looking at here." He gestured around the room, to Kellan, the Tenda clone, Kate, Sabrina, the real Tendra, the Milky Way spiraling around the room, and the tubes behind them.

"Do you know why you are both trying to protect this child, why you both put her safety above your own? Do you understand what we've been doing here yet, Tendra?"

"She's mine! She's my daughter, I know it," Tendra said.

"No, she's my daughter! Nobody better even think of coming close to her." Kate held her gun firmly on Ringbak while Sabrina moved from behind her back and into the center of the room.

"Tell them, child. Tell them what you are," the AI commanded.

Sabrina looked deep into Kate's eyes, then looked at Tendra. "You're both my mother. I am both of you, and some of him as well," she said, looking toward Kellan, "and some of him," she looked toward Ringbak, "and all of them," she said, looking deep into the Milky Way.

"That's right, child, and it is your time to take control," Mother spoke.

"Who's that? Who's there?" Kate demanded.

"She is in control, she is in charge, Agent Pierce. Please put your weapon down, it won't work in here."

Tendra lost control of herself, she felt it, she was exhausted, confused, so confused even though the words all made sense.

"No!" she screamed with blood-curdling volume. "I can't do this anymore. You want a reset, fine. Kill me. Take my life now so that I don't have to see any more of this. I want this all to be over, right now, kill me!" she sobbed, her tears falling. They burned into the floor as everyone watched.

Ringbak dropped to the floor as well, everyone fell, except Sabrina. Marone started ripping at his clothes first, followed by Ringbak.

"It's hot, stop it, stop this, what are you doing? Make it stop," Ringbak commanded. He stood again, reached out with his arm toward Tendra, and she began to choke, dropping her knife. She couldn't breathe.

Kellan scrambled for her. "Tendra!"

She looked into his eyes. It felt good to be that close to him one last time. *Goodbye, my love*, she thought to herself, *I will love you always.*

Kellan took the knife from her hand and stood up. Clenching it, he thrust it into Ringbak's neck, spilling his blood and his life all over the pristine, white floor.

Mother screamed, "No! What have you done?"

Tendra regained herself and pulled the knife from Ringbak's's neck and threw it hard into the forehead of Marone, killing him instantly.

Kate fired her gun at Tendra, but Kellan stepped immediately in front, protecting her and taking the bullet for himself. Tendra dropped to his side and held him in her arms as he bled, again.

The room began to vibrate, the ship rattled, and a hum permeated the walls. Tendra knew that sound, it was the engines coming to life. Kellan stumbled to his feet, clutching the wound in his abdomen. He grabbed Marone's badge from his cold fingers and pressed it up against three markings on the wall. Three doors opened.

"What is this?" Tendra scanned the doors. "Are those–"

Kellan moved quickly and pushed Tendra into one, then grabbed Sabrina and tossed her into another. Kate ran to them, but both doors closed before she could reach them.

As Tendra's eyes closed, she could hear Kellan's last words, "Get in if you want to see your daughter again. Hurry."

Tendra was in a pod, and she felt it break away and fall back then float effortlessly beside the ship.

The pod next to her rotated and she could see Sabrina's scared face inside.

The room disappeared in front of Kate as she floated back. She saw Kellan at a wall, pulling on something large, something mechanical just as the room filled with blinding light.

She was in a lifepod, leaving the ship. In front of the ship, a large disruption was building up. Kate saw a fuzziness in front of her, around her. She felt her body being pulled toward the hole while the pod moved away from it. What looked like a wormhole swirled around like water spinning around a drain. Colors emitted from the inside, and sparks danced around the outside. It spun and turned rapidly. A tunnel opened briefly just before the ship disappeared into it.

Kate watched as the ship left through the hole and the hole disappeared as she got further away. She looked through the glass as best she could, but there was no sign of the other two pods.

Kate saw the fire around her pod and felt the heat as it burned into the atmosphere. Her pod spun rapidly. She felt herself fading, the pressure in her head too much to handle. She went out.

The hatch to the pod opened quickly, steam surrounding it. Kate woke up and climbed out. She was in a thick, covered jungle.

She heard a rustling in the brush and fished for her sidearm but it was gone. She climbed up over a rotted tree and was met by Tendra, standing there in makeshift clothing, her hair braided and scars spread across her bare midriff. A small group of children surrounded her, wearing similar makeshift clothing. Their half shirts revealed their identity. They were hybrid children.

One of them spoke, a girl, "Are you here to help us?"

"Where is here?" Kate wanted to know.

"We have been waiting for you," Tendra said.

"Waiting, what do you mean? How long was I out?"

"We all left at slightly different times, Kate, and the portal created some kind of time interference, I don't know, but I've been down here a full year waiting for you to land."

"Sabrina! Where's Sabrina?"

"I saw her pod hit the atmosphere a few months after mine, but it went clear across the sky. She could be thousands of miles away, I don't know. We'll find her."

Kate was confused again, but something felt odd. The space distortion she saw when the wormhole appeared made her think and ask, "Wait, where are we? What's going on here, a whole year has passed?" She could tell by Tendra's face that there was more going on.

Tendra knelt down toward Kate, smiled, and filled her in, "Kate, the ship created something. The tunnel it went through in space, it caused–"

"What? It caused what?"

"Time dilation. It's called time dilation."

"How long?"

"It's been ten years since we went up to the ship."

THE
END

Made in the USA
Columbia, SC
10 February 2022

55857559R00174